ALOHA ALIBI

Charlotte Gibson Mysteries #1

JASMINE WEBB

Prologue

The longest-lasting relationship I'd ever had was with my Netflix subscription's true-crime shows, and I was the kind of person who fell asleep listening to *My Favorite Murder*, but the first time I had a gun shoved in my face, I still felt this huge urge to pee myself.

Don't wet your pants. If he shoots you, you're going to smell like pee when they find the body. If you have to be a corpse, be a sexy one. No one thinks urine is sexy. Except maybe a certain rapper.

Well, it was good to know my brain had its priorities in order.

Okay, why don't we focus on not getting murdered instead? I asked myself as I put my hands up.

"All those diamonds, in the bag, now," the man in front of me ordered, shoving a plain black duffel at my chest. I grabbed it and immediately began doing as he ordered, scooping up diamond rings by the handful and shoving them in, trying to avoid glancing up at the menacing muzzle pointed at my chest.

"All right, all right," I said in what I hoped was a calm voice. "Whatever you want."

The man in front of me had pulled a pretty transparent stocking up over his face that didn't hide all that much, and while I worked, he looked up at the security camera, pointed the gun at it, and shot it out. An involuntary squeak escaped my mouth at the sound.

"Faster," he ordered.

"Trust me, we both want this to go as fast as possible," I replied, the words coming out of my mouth before my brain had a chance to decide it was a bad idea. Great.

"Shut up," the man spat. "Seriously, shut up and give me what I want."

I rushed over to the next cabinet and began trying to unlock it, but given the pressure of the situation, my hands shook as I went to slip the key into the lock.

"Come on!" the man shouted, shooting the gun above me, the bullet smashing the mirror behind into a thousand pieces. Small bits of glass cascaded over me.

"Do you seriously think that's helping?" I shouted back. Mom had always told me that one day, my big mouth was going to get me shot. I didn't think either one of us would have imagined it was while I was being robbed at work, though.

The key finally slipped into the hole, and I twisted it in the lock, pulling open another drawer, this one full of diamond-encrusted bracelets and earrings. I tossed them all into the bag then handed it back to him.

"The safe in the back," the man said. "I need you to unlock it."

"I can't," I replied, the blood draining from my face. "I don't have the code. I'm just an employee here."

"Bull," the man said. "Come on, take me to the safe."

Blood pounded in my ears as panic threatened to overtake me. He was going to kill me as soon as I didn't open the safe for him. I knew that, because even through the mask, I recognized the robber.

It was Stevie Ham, the youngest of the Ham brothers, who ran drugs into Canada, and one of Seattle's biggest screw-ups. Seriously, it was nothing short of a miracle that the guy hadn't gotten himself killed yet.

Honestly, how could one of the most recognizable crime figures in Seattle decide to rob a jewelry store without at least throwing on a mask? That was some real criminal 101 stuff right there.

And guys like Stevie Ham didn't leave witnesses.

I'd seen way too many articles in the paper about victims of the Ham brothers and their drug wars. They weren't the kind to just let people go.

If I didn't do something in the next minute or so, I'd be a corpse on the ground. Hopefully, I'd at least get a mention on my favorite podcast. Was that too much to ask?

There was only one problem: I wasn't quite ready to die just yet. So what was I going to do? I figured literally anything was better than sitting around doing nothing and waiting for the end, so I racked my brain for ideas in an attempt to stop a bullet from passing through it anytime soon.

"Come on, take me to the safe. Fast," Stevie

shouted, motioning toward the back door with his gun. I nodded, pulling out the key fob that gave me access to the back room of the jewelry shop. I quickly swiped it against the scanner and opened the door. Stevie pressed the gun against my back, which tensed immediately, and shoved me forward. This was my chance.

As soon as I'd passed through the doorway, I grabbed the heavy metal door and shoved it closed as hard as I could. Stevie's arm was still in the doorway, but the rest of him hadn't passed the threshold yet. A sickening crunch reached my ears, and he cried out in pain as his arm got stuck between the door and the jamb. He dropped the gun in surprise.

"Stupid bitch," he called out, grunting as he put his full weight against the door.

Luckily, I had known that was coming, and I wedged the edges of my sneakers against the doorframe. My idiot boss had been opposed to me wearing sneakers at work, saying that high heels were more becoming to an upper-class jewelry saleswoman.

Well, the joke was on him. My sneakers were about to save my life.

Stevie shoved the whole weight of his body against the door, but thanks to the leverage of my shoes, he wasn't able to open it at all.

While he moved back to have another go at it, I quickly reached down, scooped up his gun, and pointed it right at him as he burst through the door.

"I don't care if you leave with the diamonds. Just get out of here," I told him, aiming the gun directly at his chest. Always aim for the body. I'd watched enough true crime to know that. It was a bigger target, and I was more likely to hit something.

Not that I actually expected I'd have to *shoot* this gun. After all, I was giving the guy carte blanche to get out of here with his tens, probably hundreds of thousands of dollars' worth of diamonds.

I guess the cocaine business just wasn't as profitable as it used to be.

But instead of taking the opportunity to get out with his loot, Stevie did what any idiot with more testosterone than common sense would: he charged toward me.

"*Why do you have to be so dumb?*" I shouted as I squeezed the trigger, pressing my eyes shut involuntarily as the gun exploded in my hand. A split second later, a thud reached my ears, and I opened my eyes to see Stevie lying in a rapidly expanding pool of blood.

He wasn't moving. It didn't take an expert to know I'd killed him.

Chapter 1

Stepping off the plane at Maui's Kahului Airport was like being punched in the face by humidity. My wavy chestnut hair immediately frizzed up, and I sighed, knowing there was nothing I could do about it now.

"I guess we're not in Seattle anymore, Coco," I muttered to the happily panting dachshund–golden retriever cross in his carrier at my side.

Seriously, it was the middle of October. This was supposed to be sweater weather. Just the other day, I'd wrapped my hands around a warm latte at the Starbucks in Pike Place and people watched as I waited for my shift at the jewelry store to start, not realizing I was only a few hours away from being robbed and my entire life changing in an instant.

It wasn't just the fact that I'd killed a man. I was surprisingly okay with that part. After all, he definitely would have killed me if I hadn't killed him first, and he was just not a good dude. So yeah, there had been a few nightmares, but I had spoken with the psychologist the lead detective on the case had recommended to me, and she'd helped me to cement the fact that it wasn't my fault and to come to grips with what I'd done.

What had really changed things was when Stevie's two brothers had started coming after me. First it was just cars driving slowly past my apartment building late at night. Then one day, they actually shot bullets into the side of the building.

"We'll do our best to trace them," Detective Maria Lopez had told me, but the look on her face screamed the rest of the sentence that she didn't say out loud. "But they're experienced criminals, far smarter than their idiot brother who got shot by a jewelry saleswoman, and we're not going to find anything."

Three days after the building was shot up, I was leaving my apartment, taking Coco for a walk, and as I stepped out into the hallway, my toe kicked a box that had been left at the door. It was small, plain, and brown, and my heart leapt into my throat.

I immediately picked up Coco, barricaded myself in my apartment, and called Detective Lopez. I wasn't going to take any chances. She came over herself, and I watched through the peep hole as she squatted down, checked out the object that had been left in front of my door, then pulled out her radio and said something into it before knocking on my door.

I opened the door and let her in.

"It's a finger," she told me, and my blood froze.

"Like… a human finger?"

"It appears so."

"I'm getting out of here," I said. "That's it. I'm leaving Seattle."

"You don't have to do that," Detective Lopez told me. "We can protect you."

I barked out a laugh. "Just like you protected the dude out there with four fingers? Yeah, no thank you. I've become kind of attached to my fingers over the last twenty-eight years. I'd rather not lose one of them. Or worse."

Detective Lopez gave me a sympathetic look. "Do you have somewhere else to go?"

"Yeah," I replied. "One of my least favorite places in the world."

"WELL, IF IT ISN'T CHARLOTTE GIBSON, IN THE flesh! How's it going, Charlie?" My best friend from childhood, Zoe Morgan, stood out from the crowd waiting at arrivals. I took in her appearance, not having seen her for the last twelve years.

The awkward, bony teenager who had always crouched to make herself seem shorter than she was had blossomed into one of the most beautiful women I'd ever seen. Now at least five foot eleven, made taller by the heels she wore – high school Zoe would never have been caught dead in heels – she wore a simple, flowing white shirt and a pair of jean shorts, showing off her deep-golden-brown legs. Her afro added to her height, and her dark-brown eyes exuded warmth.

"Zoe," I said warmly, rushing toward her. She

instantly took me in a huge hug, and it was as if the last dozen years had never happened. "Thanks for coming to get me."

"Of course. I couldn't let your arrival in Hawaii be your mom telling you that you looked too thin and needed to eat something."

I laughed as I pulled away from the hug. "That's a good point. And yet I'm at least two sizes bigger than I was the last time I saw her. But look at you, Zoe. You've certainly grown into your, well, your height."

"I eventually realized that no matter how hard I tried, there was no way I'd ever be as short as you."

"Hey!"

"I mean that in the best possible way. So you're right, I embraced it. But not until I was twenty-four or so."

"You have no idea how happy it makes me to see you this happy," I said as warmth flooded through me. What was wrong with me? I wasn't normally this sappy. But Zoe had always brought that side of me out.

My parents had moved the family to Hawaii when I was seven years old. Zoe and I were in the same class in second grade. And while Zoe was kind and sensitive and liked drawing pictures of fish and crabs, the fact that she was half Black and rather shy meant that she often found herself the target of bullies.

I, on the other hand, had never been described as either sensitive or kind. But there had been one thing I hated, even as a child: bullies. When, at recess one day, I spotted Natalie Cornell kicking sand into Zoe's face, I asked her to stop. Natalie looked me right in the eye as she picked up a handful and threw it directly at Zoe.

Since Natalie seemed to like sand so much, I fed her a handful of it for lunch.

I was suspended from school for three days, but my actions sealed a friendship between me and Zoe that lasted until our family left Maui when I was sixteen.

It wasn't that we'd had a rift; it had just been harder to stay in touch back then, and life happened. But when I'd called Mom to tell her what had happened and that I was coming to stay with her for a while, she had given me Zoe's number, and my friend was the one I'd asked to meet me at the airport.

And boy, was I ever glad I had.

"So how come you've come back to the island?"

"There's a gangster in Seattle trying to kill me because I killed his brother in the course of an attempted robbery," I replied.

"You know, if anyone else had told me that, I'd call them crazy and ask the real reason, but with you, I actually believe it. You killed a gangster's brother?"

"Yeah," I replied. "Have you heard of the Ham brothers out in Seattle?"

"They're drug runners, aren't they? I heard one of them was killed the other day. That was *you*?"

"Well, to be fair, he was going to kill me if I didn't get him first," I replied. "Plus, I gave him the opportunity to run. I even told him he could take the diamonds. I mean, how dumb do you have to be to get yourself shot when you were given a free pass to finish your robbery successfully?"

"Maybe he figured the gun could be traced back to him," Zoe mused. "Who knows? Either way, I'm really glad you're okay."

"Me too."

"So you were working at a jewelry store? Is that your career now?"

"I'm not sure I'd refer to it as a career. Mom certainly wouldn't. More along the lines of the latest adventure that pays my rent. Not that sitting on a tiny stool and helping rich ladies try on diamond rings is especially adventurous. How about you? Let me guess: you studied oceanography." Zoe had always loved the sea and all the creatures that lived in it.

"No," she replied, shaking her head. "I ended up going into medicine, and I work as a doctor at Maui Memorial now."

"Wow, your life is *much* more impressive than mine," I replied. "Mom always used to comment about how I should try to be more like you. I'm sure she's going to double down on that now that you're a doctor and I'm... well, whatever the opposite of that is."

Zoe laughed. "It's not like life is a competition."

"Well, either way, you're the fancy doctor healing people, and I'm the kid eating glue in class. But then, I guess that was always our relationship."

"Please. You're the kid who saved me from bullies. Don't sell yourself short."

I followed Zoe through the parking lot to her practical five-year-old Camry. I put my suitcase in the back, Coco at my feet, and five minutes later, we were driving down the red-stained asphalt road lined with palms as old-fashioned green lamps lit the street with a warm glow. I knew if it were still daylight, the West Maui Mountains would stand tall in the distance.

"So what are your plans?" Zoe asked as we drove along. "Find another job? Are you staying here forever?"

"Frankly, I haven't thought this through beyond the fact that in Hawaii, I'm less likely to find a human finger left on my doorstep," I replied. "I guess I'll have to find a job. If I have to live with Mom for more than two weeks, I'll probably start fantasizing about Stevie Ham's brother cutting my limbs off one at a time."

Zoe laughed. "I'd offer you a place to stay, but my apartment is a tiny studio, and I'm pretty sure we'd hate each other within the week. You're probably better off at your mom's."

"What's the market like here right now?" I asked.

Zoe shot me a look. "You've lived in Hawaii. What do you think? Airbnb hasn't helped things, either."

"Great," I groaned. "So I need some cash, and fast."

"Do you not have any savings?" Zoe asked.

I leaned back in the seat and groaned. "No. It turns out I'm not good at being an adult. You probably should have guessed that when I told you I had to leave Seattle because a gangster left a finger at front of my door. I have eighteen dollars in my checking account, and Mom paid for my plane ticket over here."

"That's fair," Zoe admitted. "Okay, well, living with your mom won't be that bad, I'm sure."

"Those are some famous last words."

Twenty-five minutes after we left the airport, Zoe pulled up in front of a cute little bungalow on Kahaapo

Loop. It was painted canary yellow, with white trim and a white garage door, and the lanai at the front was hidden from the street by a row of large sago palms offering some more privacy. It was neat and tidy, exactly like my mother.

And the exact opposite of me.

"Thanks for the ride," I said to Zoe as I climbed out and picked up Coco's carrier. Even though it was October and nearly ten o'clock, it was still at least seventy-five degrees out, and I was blasted by the warm air as I stepped out of the car. Okay, maybe I'd missed the weather here a little bit.

"Anytime. Call me tomorrow. I'd love to catch up some more, and I don't work until three."

"I will," I promised.

I grabbed my suitcase, rapped the lid of the trunk a couple times to let Zoe know she was clear to reverse, then walked up to the front door.

Mom opened it right as I raised my fist to knock, because of course she did.

"Charlotte," Mom said as soon as she saw me, taking me into a big hug. "Oh, my darling daughter, it's so good to see you again. But you're so thin! Don't you know how to feed yourself up there in Seattle? Men love a woman with something to grab. More cushion for the pushin'."

"I'm not that thin, Mom," I replied with a groan. "And please never say that phrase in my presence ever again."

How had *I* ended up with the mother who liked to give her daughter sex tips?

"Oh, don't be such a prude. How do you ever expect to nab yourself a man if you won't even talk about what they like?"

"I don't mind talking about it, just not with the woman who birthed me."

Great. I'd been home all of ten seconds, and this conversation had taken a super-uncomfortable turn. I needed to get some cash, and fast.

"Of course, it's probably not going to be all that easy to find a man when you killed a gangster," Mom mused.

"It was self-defense."

"Oh, *I* know it was, but men don't find women who kill other men sexy. They'll always be wondering in the back of their mind if they'll be next if they step out of line."

"Good. That's a feature and not a bug in my opinion," I replied as I opened Coco's carrier and let her loose in the house.

"And this must be Coco," Mom said sweetly, kneeling and holding out a hand, which my dog immediately ran toward on the off chance it held treats. We were pretty similar that way, me and Coco.

"She is," I said proudly. Coco had been one of a litter of puppies my neighbor Susanne's dog had had about two years ago. That dog was a golden retriever, so it was a surprise to everyone when the puppies came out with stubby legs and floppy ears. Another neighbor, Erik, owned a dachshund that was obviously the father.

Frankly, I had a lot of questions, mostly to do with the logistics of how the puppies had been made. Was the dachshund standing on top of a chair to be able to reach? Had the golden retriever even felt anything at all?

Anyway, the details weren't important. What *was* important was that a few months later, Susanne's dog was visibly pregnant, and when the puppies were born, she decided she didn't want anything to do with them. I convinced her to let the puppies stay with the mother until they were eight weeks old and that I'd find good homes for all of them.

And I had—for four of them, at least. Coco had stayed with me.

She was the runt of the litter, only barely bigger than a regular dachshund but with slightly longer legs and a beautiful, silky golden coat. Her face was mostly dachshund, with a tiny bit of Golden Retriever in the snout. She was a bit funny looking, what with having come from a very unlikely couple breeds of dogs, but I had loved her since I'd first laid eyes on her.

"Let's get the two of you settled in, then. How was your flight? I have some leftover casserole in the fridge I can heat up for you."

"Thanks, Mom. That sounds great, actually." My stomach rumbled. The fact was, food hadn't exactly been a priority in my life since a gangster had come after me. When I was upset, I was a stress eater, and that meant I lived in the Dairy Queen drive-through. I'd had two Royal Oreo blizzards for the past two days, and not only was that not *nearly* enough food for one person, but it also might not have been the healthiest choice ever.

Whatever. The crème part of the Oreos were practically milk, and that counted as dairy. So did the ice cream.

I walked through Mom's home, which I'd never seen before. It was a standard modern bungalow, with hardwood floors, ten-foot ceilings, a kitchen that had been built with the house in the nineties, and the same furniture we'd had when I was a child.

A wave of nostalgia washed over me, and I headed to the fridge to grab a beer, only to find it empty of them.

"Don't you have anything to drink?"

"I have water, or you could have some matcha. Green tea helps you sleep, you know."

"Since when have you abandoned your good friend Mr. Budweiser?"

Mom shot me a look. "Ever since I realized how unhealthy a life fueled by alcohol can be. Have some green tea. It's good for you."

I scrunched up my nose. "Thanks, but no thanks. I guess I'll survive with water."

"Your organs will thank you."

"If they start talking, I think that means there's something very wrong."

Mom rolled her eyes at me. I really had to find my own place.

Chapter 2

The next morning, I was immediately inspired to go on a job hunt thanks to the lack of alcohol available in my mom's house and the lack of funds in my bank account to remedy the situation.

Well, I did still have eighteen dollars. I went to Long's Drugs to grab some beer. I came out of there with a twelve-pack of Coors Light and five dollars left to my name. Worth it.

I tossed the beer in the back of Mom's Corolla and drove back into Kihei. Hopefully there were jobs available in town right now. I parked a couple blocks away from the main strip and began walking down South Kihei Road, looking for signs in the windows announcing businesses seeking help.

Across from Kalama Park, among a small rag-tag group of brightly colored low-rise shops with plenty of patio space, I hit the jackpot. Aloha Ice Cream, a small shop in a bright-robin's-egg blue wooden building, had a handmade HELP WANTED sign in the window. I peered inside and quickly realized why. The woman working behind the counter was obviously overwhelmed. Tall, with sandy blond hair streaked with grey, she wore a loose blouse and flowy skirt along with a bandana to keep the hair back from her eyes—and the customers' food. This place had been here when I was a kid, and this very lady had served me ice cream back then too. There were at least three families, with a dozen kids between them, inside the shop, and while she scooped as fast as she could, the line kept growing, and she seemingly didn't have anyone else to help her.

I snuck past the line and around the counter, where the woman barely glanced at me.

"I'm looking for a job, and you look like you need a hand," I said.

"Grab a scoop and start working. Price list is behind the counter; point of sale is self-explanatory. You help me get through this line without screwing up and you're hired."

This was a boss after my own heart.

I grinned and joined her behind the counter, looking out at the customers. "Who was next in line?" I asked in my perky customer service voice, plastering a smile on my face.

I'd gone from terrible retail job to terrible retail job in the past. If there was one advantage to never having started on a "real career," it was that I could hop into a new customer-facing position as if I'd been born popping out of a cash register.

"I want a sample spoon of maple hazelnut," a woman in a hot-pink jumpsuit said, waddling up to the display cabinet. Just beneath the counter was a ton of boxes of sample spoons, and I happily grabbed one and handed the woman a sample.

"I also want to sample the triple chocolate."

Seven sample flavors later, she finally settled on a triple scoop of chocolate chip cookie dough. I was relieved that I was finally going to get to serve a second customer, but she turned and grabbed the arm of a girl who looked about ten.

"Jessica! It's your turn. Come decide what flavor ice cream you want!"

Maybe this job wasn't going to be *quite* as easy as I thought.

Most of the customers I served over the next hour didn't feel the need to sample half the flavors in the shop before making a decision, and I quickly got into a rhythm of serving hungry tourists and figuring out how to use the point-of-sale machine. Eventually, around one in the afternoon, there was enough of a break that I finally got to actually introduce myself to my boss.

"You're hired," she announced as soon as the store was empty, holding out a hand, which I shook. "I'm Leslie. You used to live here, didn't you?"

"Yeah. Charlotte Gibson, but you can call me Charlie. Everyone else does. I stopped by here a few times when I was a kid."

"I remember; I caught you stealing a pint of ice cream from the freezer when you were about twelve."

"Oh, yeah, that happened," I said, awkwardly reaching back and grabbing my neck while biting my lip. I'd completely forgotten about that. "If it helps, I wasn't a born thief; Tommy Johnson said I wouldn't be able to do it, and I had to prove him wrong. But if I remember right, I got away with it."

"I let you leave the store with the ice cream, but I knew you were doing it. You weren't nearly as subtle as you thought you were. Even your mother knew; she came in later that day and paid me for the pint."

Warmth flooded my face, and I knew it was doing a pretty good impression of a tomato. "I guess we never were as subtle as we thought as kids, were we? I had no idea my mom ever found out. Anyway, I promise not to steal anything, even if Tommy dares me to do it again."

"That's unlikely, seeing as he's at Halawa."

"I guess I should have seen that coming," I said, raising my eyebrows slightly. Halawa was the largest prison in Hawaii, on Oahu. "What did he do?"

"Armed robbery. Looks like you did slightly better for yourself."

"Luckily, my life of crime started and ended with that pint of ice cream."

"I'm glad to hear it. So what brings you back to the island? I thought you'd left for good."

"Me too. I just had to get away. Not from the cops," I added hurriedly.

Leslie laughed. "Hey, it's always nice to see the island kids come back after they've left for the mainland. Too many good young people leave here for college and never come back."

"Well, I'm happy to be back. I'm looking forward to living the more relaxed island lifestyle again." It helped that no one on Maui wanted to kill me. Of course, there were some painful memories here, too. But I stamped those down. Now wasn't the time to think about them, and I wasn't about to confess to all of my trauma to my new boss.

A few minutes later customers began piling in once more, and Leslie and I stopped our conversation as we switched back to customer service mode.

"Hi there. Can I help you?" I asked a man who entered at the end of the miniature rush. He was not dressed for Hawaii at all, and it showed. Wearing a full suit—I was fairly certain I'd never seen *anyone* on the island wearing a full suit in my life—he had his phone pressed to his ear and angrily spoke into it, spittle flying from his mouth.

"No, that's not acceptable. I need to be back in New York in six hours. I don't care that the flight's longer than that. Get me a damn Concorde if you have to. They still have to be around, don't they? I've had it with this place. I'm getting a cab, and when I get to the airport, you'd better have a ticket ready and waiting for me."

I raised my eyebrows slightly. While this guy certainly seemed like he needed some ice cream—and maybe a couple Xanax—he didn't exactly give the impression he was in the mood for it. He jabbed the button on his phone to end the call then looked up at me.

"Hi. Look, my Uber account's been hacked, and I can't get into it. Any chance you can call me a cab?" the man asked, his tone calm and friendly. I was surprised at how polite he was now that he was off the phone.

"Sure," I answered, pulling out my own phone. "Hey, Leslie, what's the number for the cab company here?"

She called it out to me, and I dialed, putting my hand over the receiver while it rang.

"You just want to be picked up outside?"

The man nodded, and I gave the dispatcher our location.

As I hung up, I couldn't help but notice the man eyeing the ice cream selection, and I had to imagine it was mighty tempting, especially to someone in a full suit on a day like this.

"Can I get you a cone while you wait?"

"Yeah," he said. "Yeah, I might grab one, actually. Though I gotta get back to New York."

"So I heard. Business?" I asked.

"Yes. I was just here overnight, working on getting the financing sorted out on a construction project. That took longer than I anticipated; is it normal for people here to be so casual about things?"

"Island time," I said with a nod. "It's certainly not the same as New York time."

"No, that it's not. Anyway, I'll have a scoop of that triple chocolate. In a cup, please, so I don't spill it on my suit when it inevitably melts the instant I step outside. Though Tony would be thrilled if I had to order yet another Armani this year."

I bit back a smile as I turned to grab the cup and gave him an extra-large scoop. He seemed like he needed it, and despite the fact that he was obviously stressed to hell and back, he wasn't treating me like complete crap. That was always a plus when working retail.

He paid for the ice cream and stood near the window while he ate it, impatiently awaiting the cab's appearance.

When it showed up a minute or so later, the man thanked me again and practically ran toward it.

A couple of teenagers chose that moment to enter the shop, and I didn't think about the guy from New York for the rest of my shift.

AN HOUR LATER, AROUND FOUR, LESLIE TOLD ME I could head on home. She opened the till and counted out some cash, handing it over to me. "I'll get you to sign the official paperwork tomorrow, if that works for you."

"Sure," I said, happy to have more than five dollars to my name. "Thanks again for the job."

"Your mom is good people, and you're obviously a fast learner. I'm happy to take a chance on a local kid who's come home," Leslie said with a smile. "But don't think you're entitled to free pints of ice cream. I won't say no if you want a cone per shift, though."

"Thanks," I said. "I might actually take you up on that. The cookies and cream looks delicious."

"It is," Leslie replied. "I even make the cookie dough myself."

"Oh, I didn't realize you make all the ice cream here."

"My daughter Samantha makes it all," Leslie replied. "She's a night owl, so she comes in around midnight and is gone in the morning by the time I open the shop. That's why we're always so busy; that home-made touch makes all the difference."

I grabbed myself a small scoop, and my eyes widened as I tasted it.

"No kidding. I can understand why. This is even more delicious than I remember from when I was a kid."

"Probably because you actually earned it this time," Leslie said with a grin. "Are you good to come in tomorrow at around ten?"

"Sure," I nodded. "Thanks again."

I held up my ice cream cone in salute, threw my sunglasses back on and headed out into the Maui afternoon.

South Kihei Road was the main thoroughfare through town, so even though traffic here wasn't rare, it still seemed more backed up than I would have expected. Cars crept along, but even counting tourists who drove well below the speed limit a lot of the time, this was exceptional. Had there been a car accident up ahead?

Having nothing better to do, I decided to go investigate. I licked at my cone—it really was some of the best ice cream I'd had in my life—trying to devour it before the sun melted it too much. I found myself joining a crowd of people headed toward the north end of Kalama Park.

Flashing red and blue lights in the distance told me

that sure enough, an incident requiring the presence of the authorities had occured. As I got closer, I had to push through the crowd of idle onlookers until I reached the yellow police tape cordoning off the entire north end of the park.

The crime scene was between two gated utility buildings at the very far north end of Kalama Park, right next to the parking lot, which had also been cordoned off. A single cab was parked in the lot, the driver leaning against the hood, smoking away, oblivious to the nearby crowd. I snuck farther into the park to get a better look at what had happened and quickly realized someone had died.

A black sheet covered what was obviously a body, but when I saw what was lying next to it, my mouth went dry.

It was an empty ice cream cup in a familiar shade of light blue. The red plastic spoon I'd stuck in it less than two hours earlier lay a couple inches away, and the last few drops of melted triple chocolate ice cream spilled out onto the concrete.

The body under the sheet was the businessman from New York. It just had to be.

But what had happened? After all, he had been planning to go straight to the airport from the ice cream place. I shuffled along the police tape, apologizing as I snuck in front of people, until I got as close as I could to the cab driver. He was far enough away from the action that there weren't really any other people around.

He was native Hawaiian, about six feet tall, and at least three hundred pounds.

"Hey," I called out to him, waving my hands until I caught his attention.

He turned and looked at me. "What's up?"

"Did you pick that guy up from the ice cream place down the street?" I asked, motioning toward the body with my head.

"Sure did. What's it to you?"

"I was curious; I'm the one who served him at the ice cream shop. I thought he was going straight to the airport. He had to get back to New York."

"Yeah, dude was pretty pent up. I was surprised he stopped for ice cream."

"His Uber account got hacked, and he needed me to call him the cab since he didn't know the number."

The man chuckled. "Sounds about right. Anyway, yeah, he hopped into the cab and told me to go to the airport, fast as I could. I asked him when his flight was, and he said he'd find out on the way but that if his assistant wanted to still have a job tomorrow, it'd be soon. He looked ready to blow. Then he gets a text, and he tells me to pull over here in the park. I mean, it seemed a bit strange given how much of a rush he was in, but as long as he was paying, what did I care? He left the cab and went behind that building there. When he didn't come back after fifteen minutes, I went looking for him. And, well, I found him. So I called the cops, and I've been here ever since."

"Man, that's crazy," I said, shaking my head. "I wonder what happened. He wasn't from here; he was just on the island for a business trip, he said."

"Well, obviously he wasn't from here. Did you see

the suit he was wearing?" the cabbie chuckled. "Tragedy, really. I haven't got a clue who would have done that to him."

"Wait, someone killed him?"

"The knife in his chest makes me think so," the cabbie replied casually.

My eyebrows rose. Murders certainly weren't unheard of on Maui, but you could usually count the number of victims in a year on one hand. "Huh, go figure. Well, thanks for the chat. Hope you're okay."

The cabbie shrugged. "It's fine. Not the first body I've come across in this job. Probably won't be the last. First one with a knife sticking out of him, though. I'm just bummed the rest of my shift's been ruined, since the cops want me to hang out here."

"Right."

I walked away from the crime scene, my head whirring. I couldn't help it; I was a naturally curious person. It was what got me into trouble a lot of the time, but hey, we all had our vices.

I pulled out my phone and sent Zoe a text.

Hey. Sorry I didn't get back to you this morning. I ended up getting a job.

Congrats! Zoe replied a moment later. *Where are you working?*

That ice cream place on South Kihei in the blue building, across from the park.

The one where you stole a pint of ice cream on a dare?

How come everyone except me remembers that?

You repressed the memory because you felt so bad?

That's probably it. Anyway, one of my customers was murdered in the park after he left here.

Wait, seriously? I heard someone died there about an hour ago.

Yeah. Businessman from New York. I called him a cab.

Are you okay?

I'm good, thanks. Not the first dead body I've seen this week. I'm starting to think it might be me.

Well, try to stay out of trouble, Zoe replied, adding a winking emoji at the end.

I told her I'd be happy to meet up with her tomorrow, we organized to grab a late lunch after my shift, and I walked back to where I'd left the car that morning.

At least I still had my twelve-pack in the trunk.

Chapter 3

I walked through the door and called out to Mom, "I'm home!"

"Good. Dinner's going to be ready in a couple hours," she replied, coming out of the kitchen while wiping her hands on a towel. She looked at the eleven cans of beer I had left disapprovingly. "I guess you'd better put those in the fridge."

"Where do you want the empty one?" I asked, and she pointed me toward the recycling bin. I might have chugged it on the way up the driveway after parking the car.

"Did you hear a man was killed on the beach not far from here?"

"Yeah, I saw the body," I replied as I threw out the empty and stuck ten of the cans I had left in the fridge. I popped the last one into the freezer; in fifteen minutes, it'd be nice and cool for drinking.

"Charlie!" my mother scolded.

"What? It's not like I'm the one who killed him."

"How do you expect to find yourself a man when you're constantly surrounded by dead bodies? Men aren't looking for a woman who's into gore and death."

"First of all, I'm not constantly surrounded by dead bodies. I've seen two of them. Three if you count the finger."

"Of course I count the finger."

"And secondly, I'm not interested in finding myself a man, and I'm certainly not interested in finding myself a man who'd be scared off by a woman who just so happened to see some bodies."

I needed to get my own place, and fast.

"No man wants to think about how many dead bodies a girl has seen when he's in the middle of making a baby with her."

"And no daughter ever wants to hear her mom utter *anything* about baby making," I said, escaping to my room to grab my laptop so I could find a place to live, away from my mom and her comments about making babies with a man.

I snuggled up on the couch with Coco and opened the lid, my computer being one of the few items I'd brought to Maui with me from Seattle. It wasn't as if I owned a lot of stuff anyway.

Surely there had to be something available for rent here that I could afford. I'd take literally anything that didn't involve living with my mother.

Unfortunately, Zoe had been right when she'd said the rental market was tighter than ever. Even for a tiny ohana—a Hawaiian term for a small carriage house—I was looking at fifteen hundred a month in rent. I was making a bit of cash working for Leslie, but it wasn't enough that I'd be able to afford that. Well, I wouldn't be able to afford rent *and* food, anyway.

I sighed after an hour of fruitless searching and watched as Coco snored away on the end of the couch by my feet. "I guess we're stuck here for a little while longer, aren't we?" I muttered to her. I had to find a way to get some money and my own place. I was flirting with thirty. I couldn't live with my mom forever.

Besides, at this rate, I'd have to add one more figure to the list of bodies I'd seen if Mom kept giving me advice on how to attract men.

THE NEXT MORNING, THE MURDER UP THE ROAD WAS the only thing anyone in the ice cream shop wanted to talk about.

"Does this mean Maui is unsafe? Should I be thinking about cancelling the rest of our holiday?"

"I heard he was some sort of big shot on the mainland."

"Gang activity, from what I heard. Did you hear the brother of a big gangster in Seattle was killed not long ago, too? Maybe they're related."

I turned to Leslie when we got a break and shook my head. "I'm guessing this is all anyone's going to want to talk about for the next week, but man, I'm already tired of hearing about this guy."

"Look on the bright side: it beats everyone telling

you how nice the weather is. This news at least adds a bit of variety to the day."

"There is that," I admitted. Besides, I was actually kind of curious about the man and who had killed him. After all, I'd listened to so many true-crime podcasts, and here I was one of the last people to see a man alive before he was murdered. I was practically a part of the story. I was going to have to email the hosts of *My Favorite Murder* and tell them all about this case. If it was interesting enough, they might even read my email on air during one of the hometown mini episodes.

However, it wasn't until the end of my shift, when I met up with Zoe, that I found out I would definitely become part of the story.

"Where are we eating?" I asked. "Keep in mind that while you're on a doctor's salary, I'm on more of a dumpster diving salary."

"Don't worry," Zoe said with a light laugh. "I'm buying. You have to discover the best food truck in town. It didn't exist when you moved, and you can't live here without trying it."

"I'm always down for a good food truck experience."

Kinaole Grill was set up in what looked to have formerly been a UPS truck, now painted a gorgeous deep blue with a Hawaiian woman on the outside of it, carrying a basket of fruit and some fish. On the other side was a lush waterfall, and the background was of one of those famous Maui sunsets. A small wooden board at the front displayed the offerings.

I ordered coconut shrimp and a slice of mango cheesecake, while Zoe went for the pulled pork with guava barbeque sauce. Both plates came with generous servings of rice and salad, and we walked across the street to the beach, sitting under a koa acacia tree on the grass with our food as we watched the sun begin its slow dip toward the horizon.

"So you heard about the man who was murdered?" I asked.

Zoe nodded. "Yeah. James MacMahon, some important bigshot from the mainland. They brought his body to the hospital last night until they could fly it to Honolulu. The medical examiner wanted help from the M.E. up there, since he used to work in New York City and has a lot more experience with murders."

"I wouldn't have thought it that hard to diagnose a knife sticking out of his chest."

Zoe gave me a disbelieving look. "Don't tell me you were somehow involved in this murder too."

"You sound like my mom. No, I just served him ice cream before he died. I chatted with the cabbie who took him to the park where he was stabbed."

"Oh. How is your new job, anyway?"

I shrugged. "It's a job. Leslie seems cool. It pays money. Not enough to get my own place, though, which is disappointing. I guess I'll find something eventually."

"Yeah. There's college here. You could enroll in some classes if you find something you like," Zoe said.

I scrunched up my nose. "I'm pretty sure academia isn't really for me."

"All right, well, how about sales? You're outgoing. Surely you'd be good at that?"

"You say outgoing; other people say annoying. It's a

possibility. I'll keep my eyes open for more opportunities. Maybe I'll do some sort of side hustle. By the way, this food is *amazing*."

"Right?" Zoe said with a grin. "It's my favorite place to eat on the island. I knew you'd love it."

"This might be the best coconut shrimp I've had in my life."

"I don't doubt it."

We sat in silence as we watched the sun for a while. My eyes filled with tears, and when Zoe looked over at me, she wrapped an arm around my shoulder. "I'm sorry. Your dad?"

"Yeah. He always loved watching the sunset, and this is the first Maui sunset since…" I let my voice trail off.

When I was sixteen, an aggressive melanoma had taken my father to an early grave. We'd left soon afterward; Mom got a job teaching in Seattle, and I swore I'd never come back to this place that had taken my father before his time. Mom moved back when she retired, but I still vowed I never would.

I had convinced myself Maui held only pain for me.

"I'm sorry you had to come back here."

"Me too. But I'm glad you're here. And I'm glad you don't hate me for falling out of touch basically immediately. It was just too hard."

"Don't worry. I completely understand. I was a bit pissed at first, but I mean, I was a teenager. I got over it, and as I got older, I understood why Maui was just too much for you."

I nodded, blinking back tears. "I'm glad one of us grew up."

"Oh, come on," Zoe said with a laugh. "You've got to be a *little* more mature than when we were teenagers."

"I walked past the Hele station earlier, and gas was three sixty-nine a gallon. I nodded and audibly whispered 'nice.'"

Zoe laughed. "Okay, so you're still mentally twelve. I guess some of us have to be."

I grinned. "You know it."

Zoe's eyes widened as she checked her phone. "Whoa."

"What is it?" I asked, peering over to look at her screen.

She handed me the phone. It displayed a tweet from a local news station. *Maui murder victim's family offers $100,000 reward for finding his killer.*

"Cool," I said with a grin.

Zoe shook her head. "No, absolutely not. There's no way you're going to solve this murder."

"I dunno. A hundred grand would certainly get me out of Mom's house sooner rather than later. That would pay for a lot of rent."

"Are you kidding me? You were just about killed by a gangster literally days ago."

"That was different; he was trying to rob me, and then his brother wanted to avenge his death."

"Right. This person has even *more* reason to kill you if you try and find them, because you'll be trying to put them in jail."

"Po-tay-to, po-tah-to."

"That's not what that phrase means at all," Zoe said,

exasperation written all over her face. "Seriously, this is a bad idea."

"Do you know how many episodes of *My Favorite Murder* I've listened to? Trust me, I'm probably more qualified to look into a murder than half the cops on this island."

Zoe raised a skeptical eyebrow. "How many of those episodes involved people who discovered the killer's identities being murdered themselves?"

"Only a few," I replied cheerily. "Besides, I won't be one of them. I'm going to be too good at this."

"Well, at least you're humble enough to see your shortcomings," Zoe said with a crazed laugh. "I mean, you're a grown woman. I won't stop you from doing this, but I do think it's a terrible idea."

"You've always been the practical one of the two of us. If I get myself seriously injured, will you stitch me up?"

"Of course I will," Zoe said. "But you'd better not let that happen."

"I don't plan on it, but you know what they say in Girl Scouts: Always have a backup plan."

"You were never in Girl Scouts, were you?"

"No. How can you tell?"

"Apart from the fact that you've never been prepared for a single thing in your life?"

"I prefer to think of myself as always being prepared for a new adventure."

"You always were the fun friend."

"Hey, you're fun too. You're just fun in a different

way. The 'girl who watches *Jeopardy!* every night and can name all the fish in the ocean' type of fun."

"Well, not *all* of them. But yes, I do still love the ocean. I took up surfing a few years ago."

"That's much more badass than anything I do."

"Come join me one morning. I'll teach you the basics. And it's less dangerous than hunting a murderer."

"Maybe," I said with a smile, but a sinking feeling grew in my stomach. Dad had always wanted to teach me to surf, and I'd always said no. "Thanks. For everything. It's easier being here when I know I have a friend."

"Of course."

"So…" I continued after a couple minutes of agreeable silence. "Did you find out anything else about the murdered guy last night?"

"You're impossible," Zoe said, swatting at me with a laugh. "I only know he's from New York."

"Hm, that's too bad. I know that, too. If his family put out a statement, I guess they know who he is. I'll be able to look into him that way."

"I heard he's some sort of property developer, but I'm not sure of the details."

"Yeah, he said he was here getting financing organized on some sort of construction project," I said. "Is there anything big in the works anytime soon?"

"Oh," Zoe said, her eyes widening. "I wonder if he's involved in the new resort project."

"What's that all about?"

"There's a company from New York that's trying to turn Kihei into Wailea North."

Wailea was the town just south of Kihei, and despite geographically being only a couple miles away, it might as well have been on Mars. Where Kihei was popular with families and had a fairly relaxed vibe, Wailea was home to the fanciest and most expensive resorts on the island.

"Are they really?"

"Yeah, and they want to tear down locals' homes to do it. They want to take over Kinolio Park and have bought up thirty of the properties behind it, expecting to tear them down to build their resort. They're also trying to get the local government to agree to move the start of South Kihei Road so that their guests don't have to cross it to get to the beach."

"That's ridiculous," I spluttered. "I played soccer in Kinolio Park."

"Well, once you go to the meetings and tell them *that*, there's no way they'll allow it," Zoe said with a cheeky grin.

"You know what I mean."

"I do. And I'm opposed to the project, too. There needs to be green space for the kids growing up here, not just beach space. And it's already hard enough for locals to find places to live; I don't want to see thirty houses torn down to build a mega luxury resort on top of that. Besides, it would totally kill the vibe of this place. Kihei is Kihei. There's nothing wrong with people wanting luxury vacations, but I like the more family-friendly feel we have in this town. If they want to build another mega-resort, they can do it in Wailea."

"Agreed," I said. "I didn't realize that was happening."

"No, you wouldn't have if you don't live here," Zoe said. "But it's caused a lot of controversy on the island. Accusations of people getting paid off, that sort of thing. The project was approved by council a couple weeks ago."

"All I'm hearing is lots of reason to murder a dude."

"I mean, people have been killed for less. I don't disagree."

"There we go. I'm five minutes in, and I've already found a motive. This is going to be a piece of cake."

"I'd rather a piece of cake than pieces of your dismembered body spread around town," Zoe replied.

"Same. But don't worry. As soon as I figure out who it is, I'll let the cops know and collect my reward. That way, I can get away from my mom and her weird sex tips." I shuddered at the thought as Zoe laughed.

"Well, it's better than bemoaning the fact that you haven't given her grandchildren yet, like mine is."

"Nope, listening to your mom say the phrase 'more cushion for the pushin'' is *far* worse, believe me."

Zoe scrunched up her face. "Okay, that's bad."

"Does your mom really want you to have kids? You're a doctor, for goodness' sake. You have to build up a career first. Are you seeing someone?"

Zoe shook her head. "Very happily single."

"Me too. I have terrible luck with men. And jobs. And life. I think I'm starting to see a pattern."

Zoe chuckled. "Come on, it can't be *that* bad."

"One guy I dated wanted me to shout out different dinosaur names during sex. I learned more about dinosaurs when I was with him than I ever did as a kid."

Tears streamed down Zoe's face she was laughing so hard, and eventually she snorted and held up a hand. "Wait, so you're saying this happened once and you didn't immediately dump him?"

"Look, I've already admitted my love life is a dumpster fire. You don't have to rub it in."

"How long did it last?"

"Three weeks. We had a fight over the fact that all the dinosaur names I learned were from the Jurassic period, and he wanted more variety. He broke up with me."

I hung my head as Zoe shrieked with laughter. "You're not serious. Dinosaur Man dumped *you*? Where's your sense of dignity?"

"A pterodactyl stole it," I muttered with a laugh. "To be fair, I was, like, twenty-one. If it happened again, I'd leave him immediately."

"I would hope so, but then I also hope there's only one guy out there who wants his girlfriends to scream out the names of dinosaurs during sex."

"A very good point."

"Well, we can grow old and be spinsters together," Zoe said. "Although we're not even thirty yet. Still plenty of time to find a man, despite the fact that my mom's acting like everything down there's going to shrivel up and die if I don't use it soon."

"I should try and find someone to hook up with who

has an extra bedroom," I mused, but Zoe shook her head.

"Nope. After hearing that story I'm pretty sure you'd find the weirdest guy on the island and nothing else. There's got to be at least one guy out there whose dream is to find a woman who will dress up as an octopus in the bed for him, and you don't want to get away from your mom *that* badly."

"That's probably true," I replied. "I guess I'll have to settle for the hundred grand and finding the killer."

Chapter 4

As soon as I got home that night, I opened my laptop and did some research on the new resort Zoe had mentioned. It was pretty easy to find—the new development wanted to keep the Kinolio name, except instead of being a nice park for kids and families to play in, with a residential neighborhood behind, they wanted to change it to Kinolio Resort—"where the sun meets the sea." Barf. I rolled my eyes at the clichéd slogan.

I mean sure, Maui sunsets *were* pretty epic, but still. Lame.

It seemed as though every archived edition of the local paper had letters to the editor from locals ranting their disapproval of the project. And yet, at every stage, it had been approved by local authorities. I couldn't help but be inherently suspicious. Had money passed between hands under the table? That sort of thing wasn't completely unheard of, although it was often never proven.

Next, I opened my Facebook account and started

searching for local groups. It didn't take long before I found one – MAUI LOCALS AGAINST KINOLIO RESORT. There were 462 potential suspects in the group. The group was public, so I didn't even need to join to read the conversations.

There was one rule to the internet I tried to abide by constantly: don't read the comments. Never, ever read the comments.

I felt dumber after about fifteen seconds of scanning.

Even in a group in which I agreed with the entire premise of the group's existence, people still managed to argue, complain, and generally post so terribly that I wanted to throw my computer across the room.

There was the one guy whose posts in the group were practically illegible: *Deeez kooks wanna bild there rezort on dis land, dey got enother ting koming to dem. Maui been ma hommmmme since I was six, no more big rezorts.*

My eyes glanced over at the name of the person who had posted that, and I raised my eyebrows. I'd gone to high school with him. Kevin Mondale had a small head and the IQ of potato. It figured the guy wasn't able to string two words together without misspelling both of them.

Then there was the woman who obviously had no idea how Facebook worked. She'd tried to share private content to the group that would show up as unavailable, had shared the same post at least three times, and, at one point, apparently attempted to upload a photo but failed to figure out how it worked. She also signed all of her posts with "sincerely, Judith." From an outsider's perspective, it was pretty cute, but I'd hate to be the child of hers that she'd be calling up constantly for help with the internet.

However, scrolling through post after post after post, I found one man who commented on every single post about the new development. He was always civil—by internet standards, anyway—but he was obviously upset about the development going ahead, and in one comment, he mentioned having heard a rumor that an executive in the development company was coming to the island.

Even if the rest of the comments hadn't gotten my attention, that one certainly would have. I looked over at the name: Charles Buchanan. Didn't ring a bell. I clicked the profile and found myself looking at a picture of a middle aged guy, probably in his mid-forties. He'd obviously taken the selfie from the front seat of his car. He wore dark-tinted sunglasses and a University of Hawaii cap on his head. He was heavyset, with short-cropped dark hair and a mustache. Scrolling through his profile, he didn't seem to have a lot of friends. Most of his posts were political in nature, mainly relating to stuff happening in the state. He didn't seem to care much for federal politics, and each post had one or two likes, tops.

If he'd shared anything more personal, it had to be set to friends only, because I didn't see it. I looked to see if there was an employer listed for him, and sure enough, he worked as a shelf stocker at a local grocery store. Perfect.

THE NEXT MORNING, I GOT UP EARLY—MUCH EARLIER than I really wanted to—and borrowed Mom's car, driving over to the grocery store where Charles worked. I stifled a yawn as I watched the front door, waiting for him to appear. I really, *really* hoped he had been working last night and that I hadn't missed the end of his shift, because otherwise, I would have gotten up at five in the morning for nothing.

And there was nothing worse than getting up early in the morning for nothing.

As half an hour passed and then an hour, my eyes drifted toward the nearby Starbucks that was just opening for the morning. I craved a caffeine hit. If someone offered me an espresso-shot IV right now , I'd be sticking it directly into my veins.

I wasn't here for coffee, I reminded myself. I was here to find Charles. Coffee could come after. And luckily, about five minutes later, he came out of the grocery store. Sure enough, he looked to weigh about two hundred and fifty pounds and held a light jacket under one arm while he lit a cigarette with his free hand. I looked him up and down. I could definitely take him in a fight. If nothing else, I could easily outrun him. He looked like he'd be completely puffed in about ten steps.

It was at this very moment that I realized I probably should have come up with a better plan than "stalk the guy and hope it works out."

I mean, I had the first part nailed down. If only I'd thought about the second point a little bit more before I'd gotten here.

Luckily for me, Charles looked up at the Starbucks and went inside.

"Yes," I whispered to myself, darting away from the car and toward the store. At least this way, I was going to come out of this with a Frappuccino if nothing else.

I casually strode into the store and stood in line behind Charles. My heart raced as I tried to figure out my next step. Should I just confront him? Accuse him of murder? Should I try and strike up a casual conversation? I had no idea.

He ordered a latte. A moment later, I placed my order and then walked to the other side of the room, where Charles was waiting for his coffee. Two older women were already there, talking quietly to one another.

I had to do something, or I was going to get nowhere.

"Did you hear about that guy who got murdered yesterday?" I asked casually.

Charles looked over at me, taken aback for a second that I was talking to him. "I did," he replied. "I heard it was a scumbag involved in that new development. If that's the case, then good riddance to him."

I raised my eyebrows. "Not a fan of the new hotel?"

"No. I grew up here. This is my home. I played in that park as a kid, and my kids play there now. I don't want it to turn into yet another gaudy monstrosity for tourists with more cash than sense. You ask me, the guy got what he deserved."

"I couldn't agree more," one of the older women chimed in. She had curly hair dyed red, and big brown eyes. She wore a pair of sensible pants and a light linen shirt; she seemed like a no-nonsense kind of woman. "I've lived on Maui since the fifties, and you ask me, this hotel is a terrible idea. It doesn't fit in with what this community should be."

"Oh, please, Rosie," the other older woman said, rolling her eyes. This woman had on a lavender tracksuit, and huge black sunglasses propped up on her silver hair cut Hellen Mirren-style. Her blue eyes glimmered, and she was a lot taller than the first woman, standing around five foot seven. "You never did understand the economy. This is Maui. Get with the program. Why should we let the other parts of the island have all the rich tourists, and we're left with just the scraps? This hotel will put Kihei on the map as a luxury destination, and soon, we'll all be swimming in more cash than we can imagine."

"Yeah, right," Charles snorted. "The only people getting rich off this development are the fat cats in New York, like the murder victim. You and me, the people on the street, we're not going to see a dime. I guarantee you that."

"Well, you ask me, it's a shame that the man's murder might stop others from coming here and building similar projects," the second woman said with a sniff. "I'm not going to refuse money from anyone, and I think if the tourists are going to come here anyway, they should be able to live life comfortably while they're here. Besides, that park was a ratty old place anyway. The people in those homes will find a new place to live. And if they don't? Well, they'll end up somewhere else."

"That's my family you're talking about," Charles snarled, getting all up in the old woman's face.

To her credit, she didn't cower away at all. Instead, she stared him down. "That's the reality of life in this economy. There are more and more people, so more and more places that we used to enjoy have to be torn down. I liked my family home, but it was eventually bought by a developer, and now there are a bunch of condos for entitled millennials like you to live in. You don't see me complaining about it."

"I'm not a millennial," the man spat at her. "I'm a proud Gen Xer."

"Well, you should have done better in life," the old woman said. "Then maybe you'd have money to invest, and you wouldn't be so bitter about this hotel being built."

"That has nothing to do with it," Charles roared. "I hate it because I don't want the town I grew up in to change."

"Well, now you sound like a dinosaur," the old woman said. "Change is inevitable. Nothing we can do about it but embrace it, and it doesn't sound like you're embracing it at all. You ask me, that poor man didn't deserve what happened to him at all. He was just trying to help the economy."

"No he wasn't," Charles snapped, and this time, he lost control. Grabbing the old woman by the throat, he pushed her up against the wall.

I gasped. "Hey, stop it!" I shouted.

"You can abuse me all you want, but all it shows is

you have the temper of someone who might have murdered that man," the old lady croaked.

Her companion looked suitably horrified, while the staff looked on in shock, everyone seemingly at a loss as to how to react.

I looked around, trying not to panic. I'd seen enough dead people this week, and as much as I disagreed with the old lady defending the new development, I wasn't sure it warranted a sentence of death by crazy dude in a Starbucks at six in the morning.

There weren't a lot of things I could use here to defend the woman, and Charles was a foot taller than me and weighed almost twice what I did. Going at him by myself was going to be pointless. So I did what anyone who grew up watching way too much WWE on TV after school would do: I grabbed a chair from the closest table and slammed it over his back as hard as I could.

Charles collapsed to the floor, and silence filled the coffee shop. The barista dropped the cup of coffee she was holding, and her coworker, who had been taking orders, stared at me like I'd just grown horns out of my head.

Rosie immediately dropped next to Charles and took his pulse. She looked up at me. "Well, you didn't kill him, so that's good. But I do believe a phone call to the police and probably an ambulance are in order."

She pulled out her phone and casually began to dial, as if she were simply ordering a pizza.

I stood, slightly dazed, letting the chair drop from my hands. I couldn't believe I had done that. Looking over at the old woman, she held her throat but seemed otherwise unharmed.

"Are you all right?" I asked her.

"Oh, yes, I'll be fine. But when the police get here, it might be a good idea to ask them to look into whether Charles here owns a gun. I wouldn't be surprised if he happened to be the guilty party in yesterday's murder." She turned to the baristas. "Have you made his coffee yet? Because if not, I don't think he'll have it, and I could use an extra shot of caffeine. I have a feeling it's going to be a long day."

These two women were crazy. One of them had barely batted an eyelid when I'd clobbered a grown man with a chair, and the other one was trying to get his coffee for free after nearly being choked to death by him. Who *were* they?

"Yes ma'am," the barista said, all the color having completely left her face. "Do you need a glass of water or something?"

"Oh, please, I've had lovers choke me harder than that," she replied with a wave of her hand.

I choked, quickly covering it up with a cough.

The barista obviously didn't know what to do with that statement either, because the blood returned to her face with a vengeance, quickly turning it to the shade of a tomato, and she hid herself behind the coffee machine once more.

"Who are you, anyway?" I asked.

"What's it to you?" the old lady asked quietly, narrowing her eyes at me. "I could ask you the same thing. You came in here making conversation with

Charles to try and goad him into telling you about the murder, didn't you?"

"I did no such thing," I replied, mustering as much outrage as I could while trying to hide the fact that I'd come here to do exactly such a thing.

"Oh, please," Rosie said. "Of course you did. Now, let us tell you something, young lady. We're going to get that reward money. A spring chicken like you doesn't have a chance, so give up now."

"Excuse me?" I asked, my indignation taking over. "You really think you two old ladies are going to solve this case on your own?"

"Of course we are. Just because we're old doesn't mean we're useless," Rosie sniffed. "So we're warning you: stay out of our way, or you'll be sorry."

Did I seriously just get threatened by an octo-genarian?

"Here's the first two lattes," the barista said, hurriedly sliding a couple of drinks across the counter to Rosie and her companion.

"Thank you so much, dear," Rosie said to her sweetly. "Dorothy and I really do appreciate it, don't we, Dot?"

"That's right," Dot answered. "Aren't you just wonderful?"

A moment later, I received my coffee as well, right as a police car pulled into the lot. I was more grateful than ever for the existence of caffeine.

Chapter 5

The two cops who stepped out of the cruiser couldn't have looked more as though they'd rather be anywhere else than here. And I mean, I couldn't blame them. It wasn't even six in the morning, and there had already been an assault at a Starbucks.

At least they could probably get some free coffee out of it.

"What's going on here?" the first one asked as he stepped through the door, looking onto the scene. He was obviously the senior of the two, in his mid- to late forties, with a beer gut that practically hid his utility belt from sight completely. He stuck his thumbs into his belt buckle and looked casually around the room. He obviously wasn't very concerned.

"This woman was attacked by that man," the barista told him in a shaky voice, pointing toward Rosie and Charles, hand trembling. "Please, you have to arrest him."

The cops both looked at Charles. "Is this true?" the

younger man asked. He had to be just out of the police academy; his face was pockmarked from a bad case of acne not that many years ago.

"Well, it's all a bit exaggerated," Charles said. Obviously, the presence of the cops had calmed him down significantly. "Just a bit of a misunderstanding. And it's not like they're all innocent. That one hit me over the head with a chair," he added, pointing at me.

"Yeah, so you wouldn't kill this old lady," I replied.

"Who are you calling old?" she snapped at me.

The senior cop pinched the bridge of his nose. "All right, all right, everyone calm down. You," he said, pointing to Charles. "I recommend you forget about being hit with the chair, because it sounds like you deserved it, and if she hadn't done it, you'd be facing bigger charges. Now, which one of you was the one he attacked?"

Dorothy raised her hand as if we were in primary school. "Me."

"Do you want to press charges against him?"

"Well, I don't want a man like that running around town unchecked, but I suppose if it was just a one-time thing…" she trailed off.

"It was," Charles said hurriedly. "I'm sorry. Please don't arrest me. Or tell my boss. I was just upset. I promise it won't happen again."

"All right. If everyone agrees, I'll simply escort this man off the premises, and the rest of you can go about your day," the older cop said. "No fuss, no muss."

No paperwork, I thought to myself.

Dorothy nodded, and Charles left with the cops. I

watched as they exited the shop; the two chatted with Charles for a little bit, the older cop leaning casually against a railing, and the two older women watched the scene as well before whispering to one another.

The three men split up a moment later, with the cops going about to solve whatever other petty crimes I imagine there were to solve this early in the morning on a weekday in Maui, and I headed out the door, thinking over the scene I'd just witnessed.

In the last few minutes, I'd seen a grown man try to kill an old lady, had two geriatric women tell me they were going to beat me to the reward money, and gone full WWE on that grown man myself.

And it wasn't even seven o'clock yet.

I had certainly learned two things this morning: for one, Charles was still one of my main suspects. He obviously had a temper and wasn't afraid to resort to violence if provoked. He certainly seemed like the kind of guy who would stab a dude in a park in the middle of the day.

I had also learned that I wasn't the only person going after the cash reward. I supposed it had been pretty naïve of me to think I was going to be the only person who saw the promise of a hundred grand and thought solving a murder was a better side hustle than driving for Uber. But those two women hadn't made their way into the Starbucks by accident. They had been following Charles too. I was sure of it.

So now I faced some additional time pressure I hadn't considered: if someone else beat me to the punch

—or in this case, the killer—I could kiss that reward money goodbye.

There was nothing I could do before the end of the day, anyway. I headed to the ice cream store, parked the car, and sipped my coffee on the beach, watching the day break into a gorgeous Maui morning until it was time to open up the shop.

THROUGHOUT THE DAY, THANKS TO SOME GOSSIPING locals, I managed to get a decent amount of information about James MacMahon and what he had been doing on the island earlier that day.

Jenny Kalhoun, who I went to high school with and now worked as a waitress at the restaurant next door, told me she'd heard he had had a lunch meeting at Ferraro's, one of the fancy restaurants at the Four Seasons. That would have cost a pretty penny, and I wish I knew what that meeting was about.

Later, I found out from a random local that James had come in on the first flight from Honolulu that morning, where he had been meeting with others involved in the development. He had travelled with his assistant, and I was immediately intrigued.

"His assistant?" I asked.

The man nodded. "That's right. She was with him, by all accounts, for most of the day."

By the time James had arrived at the coffee shop, there was no assistant to be seen. I wondered what had happened to her.

"Do you know her name?" I asked.

The man shook his head. "Wouldn't have a clue."

Great. That was a bit of a dead end, but it was still a clue all the same. She was going to be tough to get a hold of either way; there was no way his assistant was still on the island, I imagined. Still, I had to find her. That was my quest for when my shift was over.

Leslie told me to head home around three, letting me know I could have the next day off, and I decided my next step was to find that assistant. She was probably long gone by now, back in New York, but I needed to know who she was and if I could get a hold of her over the phone somehow.

I also wanted to check out the Four Seasons, but I needed someone to come with me. If I was going to get a table at Ferraro's without a reservation, it would be easier if they knew they were getting butts in both chairs at the table.

Are you working? I texted Zoe, and her reply came back a minute later.

Not until nine. What's up?

Fancy drinks at Ferraro's?

Don't tell me you're still looking into that murder.

Hey, maybe I just want to have a drink with my best friend.

Your budget is more like a six-pack that fell off the back of a truck than Ferraro's.

Fine, I'm looking for info and I feel like I'm more likely to get a table without a reservation if we're a couple.

You're ridiculous. I'll pick you up in ten. Mom's place?

Yeah, give me a bit longer though. I have to have a quick

*shower after working at the ice cream store all day. I smell like
sweaty cotton candy.*

Copy that. I'll be there in about thirty.

I rushed home and jumped in the shower. After that,
I gave Coco some quick cuddles until I saw Zoe's car
pull up in front of the house.

Shouting to my mom that I'd be back later and not
to wait for me for dinner, I headed out the door and
hopped into the passenger seat.

Zoe was one of those people who could make even
the most casual clothes look elegant as anything, dressed
in shorts and a linen top. Meanwhile, here I was in the
finest threads I'd grabbed from the 'clean' pile in my
suitcase, feeling like a giraffe that had just rolled around
in a mud hole.

"All right," she said, turning her blinker on as we
headed down to Wailea. "What are we up to? It had
better not involve breaking any laws."

"No, we're just going to see if we can find the waiter
who served James MacMahon at lunch yesterday," I
replied. "I want to know who he dined with."

"Well, I guess there's only so much trouble you can
get into looking for that kind of info," Zoe said. "I'm in."

With it being midafternoon—later than the lunch
rush but before dinnertime—Zoe and I were able to get
in without a reservation, and a woman named Kelani,
with long black hair tied back into a braid, came by to
take our drink orders a moment later.

When she left, Zoe browsed the menu. "I change my
mind. I'm starving, and this looks incredible. Do you

want to share a pizza or something? Or even have one of your own?"

"As long as you're paying for it," I said with a chuckle. "I'm happy with whatever."

"Cool. You know what? Maybe get your own. Now that I've had a waft of the food from the table next to us, I'm pretty sure I'm going to inhale whatever I order on my own."

I laughed as I scanned the menu, settling on the margherita. Classic and delicious.

The waitress returned with our drinks a moment later, and when she'd finished taking our food orders, I smiled at her.

"You wouldn't happen to have served James MacMahon, the big shot in charge of the Kinolio Resort, yesterday, would you?" I asked her. "I heard he had lunch here."

Kelani glanced around carefully as if worried she might be overheard. "And what if I did?"

"Well, we're trying to find out who he was with yesterday."

"I'm afraid I don't really know anything about that," Kelani said with a wink.

"Are you sure?" I asked. "It sounds like you know."

"I mean, I might know *something*." She gave me a knowing look, and I had no idea what she wanted. Was Kelani hitting on me?

Zoe pulled a twenty-dollar bill from her purse and slid it across the table. "Anything you might have over-heard would be *very* helpful."

Great. Of course Kelani wanted a bribe. I had just been too thick to see it. Thank goodness for Zoe.

"Well, I might know he was meeting with Calvin Monroe," Kelani said to us. "He's a financing bigwig here in town, a regular. And let me tell you, he was not happy." .

"What was he not happy about?" I asked, and Kelani looked down at the twenty. Zoe slipped another bill from her purse and added it to the first.

"From the sounds of things, James had promised Calvin that his company would have a significant stake in the new resort, and James was backing out of that side of the deal."

"Oh?" I said, raising my eyebrows.

Kelani nodded, her eyes going bright with excitement. "Yeah. We get some fights here in the restaurant from time to time, but they're usually domestic. This was entirely different, all business. They hissed at each other for a while. I heard Calvin swear to the other guy— James, the one who ended up dead—that he would be sorry for screwing him out of this deal. James told him to suck it up and that he couldn't do anything about it. Calvin ended up storming off and leaving James with the whole bill."

I raised my eyebrows. "Sounds like someone wasn't happy."

"No, he certainly wasn't. James's assistant just sat there, taking notes in her little book like nothing was the matter, either. She was a professional the whole way through."

"Do you know anything about her?" I asked. "Maybe you caught her name?"

"Sorry, not a thing, apart from the fact that she was blonde and pretty. I didn't even know who James was until I saw his picture in the paper the next day. I heard about the plan for the Kinolio Resort, of course. Everyone has. But I didn't know he was in charge of it."

I nodded. "Yeah, he was."

"Well, good," Kelani said. "I love Kihei. It has a different feel to it than here in rich resort central, a more relaxed vibe, and I'd like it to stay that way. I know you're not supposed to speak ill of the dead, and I have no idea if he was a bad guy himself, but if this stops that resort from going ahead, I'm all for it."

"Sounds like you're on the same side of this as a lot of locals."

"Of course. Sure, it's sad the guy died. But this is a whole community. He should have listened to us instead of just bribing officials until they greenlit his project."

"You think that's what happened?" Zoe asked.

Kelani nodded. "I'm positive. It's the only thing that makes sense. Two of the councilmembers for the county are going to lose their seats next election. Janice Evers is retiring, and Natalie Lee is so unpopular after voting for the project there's no way she keeps her seat. I'd be willing to bet either one of them—or both—decided to cash out while they still could."

That was certainly an interesting thought. But of course, it got us no closer to solving the murder.

"Anyway, I have to get going to my other tables,"

Kelani said, swiping the forty bucks off of ours and heading away.

"Looks like I owe you a few bucks," I said to Zoe with a grin.

She waved me away. "Don't worry about it. You can pay me back when you get that hundred grand. Although for the record, I still think this is a bad idea."

"Hey, at least I got a good suspect out of it. It sounds like Calvin Monroe wasn't happy about getting cut out of this business."

"It sure does," Zoe said. "You should try and find the assistant."

"That's what I'm spending tonight doing," I replied. "Although I expect she was on the first flight back to New York after her boss was killed."

"Likely. Still, you never know. She could be worth tracking down."

Kelani returned then with our pizzas. Honestly, this was easily the nicest meal I'd had in my entire life. The pizza, whose thin crust had obviously been cooked in a wood-fired oven, complete with a char mark or two, smelled incredible. The cutlery, with mother-of-pearl handles, had a bit of weight to it that implied quality, and the waitress even had fresh parmesan cheese to grate over the pizza if it was wanted.

For someone who was more used to McDonald's drive-through kind of service, this was next level.

"Is this how you live every day?" I asked Zoe with a grin. "With your fancy doctor's salary?"

She laughed. "Hopefully in twenty years or so, when I've finished paying off all my student loan debt. Until then, I'm living about as frugal an existence as I can. This definitely counts as a splurge."

"Well, in that case, thank you," I said, shooting her a grateful look. "I appreciate you coming out here and buying me food and drinks and bribing the waitress."

"You've been here less than twenty-four hours, and already you're being a bad influence," Zoe joked. "At this rate, you'll have me stealing ice cream from your place of work in less than a week."

"Nope. My days of being a hardened criminal are over. I had completely forgotten about that."

"Really? You offered to share the pint with me after you stole it, and I refused until you told me you paid for it. We ate it on the beach, you told me the truth about where you got it, and I threw sand at you."

I laughed. "That's right. I remember now. Wow, that's going back."

About half an hour of happy reminiscing later, the two of us headed back to Zoe's car.

"So, you're really doing this, huh?" Zoe asked as she started the engine.

"Well, I'm not going to be able to give you your forty bucks back if I don't."

Zoe shot me a look. "If forty bucks is the price it takes to keep you safe from a murderer, that's a price I'm willing to pay."

"Just out of curiosity, what's the maximum figure you would go for?"

Zoe rolled her eyes at me.

"I have to tell you about these two crazy old ladies

that I met this morning, too. They're also going for the reward money. I'm sure of it."

"I love how you choose to describe other people as crazy when you're doing exactly the same thing, making you at least as nuts as they are."

"No way. They play this role of being kindly old ladies, but then when we couldn't be heard, one of them hissed at me to stay out of their way."

Zoe laughed. "So now you're being threatened by the elderly?"

"Well, when you put it that way, it sounds ridiculous."

"That's because it *is* ridiculous. You have a job. Save some money and figure out what you want to do with your life like a normal person."

"I want to get out of my mom's house as soon as possible, that's what. And the ice cream store doesn't pay enough for me to do that."

"Well, I'm not your mother, so I won't keep telling you to stop doing it, but don't get yourself murdered. By the killer or by old ladies who think you're getting in their way."

"I'll do my best," I replied as Zoe dropped me back off in front of my mom's house. "Thanks for coming with me. And for figuring out Kelani wanted a bribe."

"One day, you'll be as street smart as me," Zoe replied with a wink and a grin, and she sped off as I headed to the front door.

Chapter 6

As soon as I got in, Coco, probably feeling neglected, started begging for a walk.

"All right, let's go for it," I said in a perky voice, grabbing her leash and calling out to Mom that I'd be back in a little bit. Coco sprinted toward the door, her little tail wagging furiously. As Coco and I walked down toward the beach, I pulled out my phone and began doing some more research, trying to find out exactly who James MacMahon's assistant was.

It didn't really take all that long to get a name. Alice Doherty was connected to James MacMahon on LinkedIn and listed as his personal assistant. And sure enough, she fit the description of being pretty, with blonde hair. Easy as pie. The harder part was going to be getting in touch with her.

She was twenty-seven, according to her LinkedIn profile, which meant there was a pretty good chance she was still using Facebook. I searched her name then searched her name along with city targeting, and still came up empty. There were about eight thousand Alice Dohertys on Facebook, and six thousand of them lived in New York City. Add to that, a thumbnail-sized photograph really wasn't enough to compare to the professional headshot on her LinkedIn profile, and I was out of luck. If I wanted to try and narrow it down further, I was going to need my laptop, on which that sort of thing was easier.

Instead, I switched over to Instagram. I figured she probably had an account, but I found Instagram's search function even more annoying to use than Facebook's. Again, no luck. I frowned then spent the next twenty minutes throwing sticks for Coco along the beach.

When we got back, I grabbed my laptop and went back to my search. It took about forty minutes, but by searching on LinkedIn for some of Alice's coworkers and then looking *them* up on Facebook and checking out their lists of friends, I managed to find her profile.

Stalkerish? Maybe just a little bit. But it wasn't as if I had bad intentions. I was just trying to find out who'd killed her boss and maybe have a conversation with her if she was up for it. She was in New York, anyway.

Or so I thought.

The newest picture on her profile—on the public part, anyway—was a shot from one of the local resorts, along with the caption, "Unexpectedly spending longer than planned in Hawaii. Will let you all know when I'm back in New York. RIP James, you were a great boss, and a better person."

I raised my eyebrows. It appeared Alice hadn't gotten right back on the next flight over after all. And, better than that, I actually recognized the beach where she'd taken that photo.

That was the beach at the Maui Diamond Resort, another one of the incredibly exclusive places in Wailea where five hundred bucks a night got you one of the cheapest rooms—if you showed up in the off season, anyway. That was my new plan for the following day: I was going to find Alice Doherty, and I was going to convince her to help me figure out who had wanted her boss dead.

DESPITE IT BEING MY DAY OFF, I STILL GOT UP relatively early, just after eight. I groaned when I looked at the time on my phone, grabbed my pillow, shoved it over my head, and tried to get back to sleep.

It was a pointless endeavor, however. Apparently, my brain was raring to go on the quest to find Alice Doherty.

"Are you taking my car again today?" Mom asked when I headed into the kitchen and poured myself a bowl of cereal.

"If you don't mind," I replied.

"Of course I don't mind. I was planning on getting groceries later, though."

"I can leave it here if you'd like."

"No, no, don't worry about it. Just be back before late, okay?"

"Sure thing, Mom."

"You know, I don't want to put pressure on you or

anything, but if you're going to live on the island for good, you're going to need to find something that pays better than the ice cream shop."

"I know," I replied with a sigh. "I'm working on it, Mom. I have a few irons in the fire." Okay, that was a little white lie.

"Well, good. The ice cream shop is a great place to start. I bet you're meeting a number of interesting men there."

"And women, too," I replied cheerily.

"Yes, well, you wouldn't move in with a woman."

"Roommates are a thing, Mom."

"Right, right. Well, you know, if you found a man who'd be willing to pay for you to have your own place, that wouldn't be the worst thing in the world, either."

"You're right, Mom," I replied, deadpan. "I think I'll go into prostitution. Great idea! Thanks!"

"You know that's not what I mean," my mom said, her hands going to her hips. "You're welcome to stay here for as long as you need, of course, but I just think you'd be happier if you had a man at your side."

"No, *you'd* be happier if I had a man at my side. There's a significant difference."

"Men aren't the enemy, Charlotte."

"No, but pushy moms who want to become grandmas are," I replied. "But you're right. If I find the right man for me, I'll make sure he pays for my lifestyle."

Mom sighed. "All right. Well, have a great day, sweetie. Try to stay out of trouble, okay?"

"I will," I lied, rinsing out the now-empty bowl of cereal and putting it in the sink.

"I was going to take Coco with me to the beach today. Is that all right with you?"

"Sure. She likes to dig holes in the sand, so she'll love you for it. I'll see you later."

I hopped into the car and drove down to Maui Diamond Resort. Once again, I decided to park a few blocks away—not only did Mom's car not exactly fit the décor, but I also didn't want to pay forty bucks for the valet parking. Then I walked up the long drive leading to the resort. Passing between the enormous Roman columns that lined the entrance, I entered the lobby, which was all high ceilings and neutral colors. Light beiges and off whites dominated the space, while floor-to-ceiling windows allowed in copious amounts of natural light. A well-manicured indoor tropical garden to the left, complete with a soft waterfall, added a touch of color, and in front of me to the right a bit was the large desk for checking in and out.

I strode up to it to find myself greeted by a friendly woman in her thirties with her hair tied back and her uniform immaculate.

"Good morning. Welcome to Maui Diamond Resort. How can I help you?"

"Yes, I'm wondering if you could please tell me which room Alice Doherty is staying in," I answered.

The woman didn't even bother looking at her computer. "I'm sorry, I'm afraid we don't have any guests by that name currently staying with us."

I frowned. "Are you sure? I know she's staying here."

"My apologies. I'm afraid you must have the wrong hotel."

"Okay, thanks," I said. As I walked away, I knew she was lying, and then it hit me as to why. I must not have been the first person who had come in looking for Alice. I kept forgetting that with the hundred thousand dollars available, there had to be others—in fact, I'd met two of them just the other day—and that half the island was probably trying to get a hold of Alice.

Crap. This was going to be harder than I'd first anticipated. I cursed myself for not thinking this was going to be a problem sooner.

I briefly considered sitting in the lobby for a few hours on the off chance that she would come down here and I could introduce myself, but quickly decided that was a stupid idea. The odds were too low, and I didn't want to waste the entire day sitting around a hotel in hopes that the person I wanted to talk to would come down to the lobby.

I was going to have to come up with a much better plan than that if I wanted to find out what room Alice was in.

Sneaking a look at the resort's computers was obviously out. For one thing, there were at least seven staff members behind the desk at all times. On top of that, the whole place was swimming in security cameras, and in a place like this, I bet they were all constantly under surveillance, too. No, I had to think of something else.

I got up and walked around the public area of the resort. I wanted not only a good idea of the layout of the place, but I also hoped that something I saw would give me an idea as to how I was going to find Alice's room.

The hotel had a long hallway leading toward the myriad of conference rooms in which they hosted some of the biggest gatherings on the island. I walked casually down it, trying to look as though I belonged, making a mental note of everything I saw. I felt like part of the crew in *Ocean's Eleven*, staking out the casino before robbing it, except of course I was only trying to find one of the guests here, not to rob the main underground safe that contained millions of dollars.

I passed a worker pushing a cart filled with boxes, and as I excused myself to pass her, I couldn't help but notice the boxes were filled with brand-new work uniforms. A few feet past her was a public bathroom, and I ducked inside.

After all, if I could get one of those uniforms, I'd be able to move around the hotel a lot more freely. Thank goodness I'd thought to bring my big straw tote-style bag this morning, since it was the most I'm-on-a-beach-holiday-looking thing I owned.

I waited about fifteen or twenty seconds after ducking into the bathroom before reemerging into the hall. Sure enough, I found myself behind the woman pushing the cart once more; she was about thirty feet in front of me now.

There was only one problem: I had no way of getting to that cart and nabbing one of those uniforms without her seeing me.

I walked closer towards her. Then, when I was about ten feet away, I let out a yelp and began hobbling.

She immediately stopped and turned. "Are you all right?" the woman asked, concern etched all over her face.

"Yeah, but I think I might have sprained my ankle," I said, clutching at my leg.

"Come over here," the woman ordered, taking my arm by the elbow and leading me toward a nearby bench in the hallway.

"Thanks," I said, rolling the ankle slightly as if testing it and wincing.

"I'm going to go find you some ice. I'll be right back."

The woman sped off in the other direction. I waited until she was gone, checked to make sure there were no other staff around—or any highly visible security cameras—and I quickly strode over to the cart, grabbed one of the uniforms from the box labeled "medium," and shoved it into my bag. I hoped they were women's sizes.

About three minutes later the woman came back with a plastic bag filled with ice. "Here, this will help."

"Thank you so much," I said gratefully. "What's your name?"

"Sandra."

"I'll make sure management knows how wonderful you are," I told her. I meant it. I didn't know if she was going to get in trouble for losing that uniform, but if so, I was going to make sure there was a good review in her name coming up. I needed to talk to Alice, but I wasn't going to get anyone in trouble who didn't deserve it if I could help it.

"I appreciate it," she said.

"Luckily, I'm not sure it's completely sprained," I said, hobbling to my feet. "I'm hoping with a few minutes of ice, I'll just be able to walk it off. Thanks again."

"No problem. Do you want me to call anyone for you?" Sandra asked.

I shook my head. "I'll be okay."

Sandra smiled and nodded then continued on down the hall with her cart. I held the ice to my ankle for a couple minutes then got up and went back into the bathroom from which I'd emerged a few minutes earlier. I dumped the rest of the ice into the sink, threw out the plastic bag, and went into a stall to change into the uniform I'd picked out.

The uniform was embroidered with "housekeeping" on the front, consisting of a comfortable yet fitted top that reminded me of a fancy version of hospital scrubs, and matching pants. They were a little bit on the large side, but it wasn't so bad that it would be noticeable.

Standing in front of the mirror, I decided to change my appearance as much as possible. My hair had been down, so I tied it back into a slick ponytail. I was only wearing lip gloss when I came in, but luckily, I had a tube of coral lipstick in my purse, which I carefully applied, along with a bit of mascara.

A super spy I was not, but in my defense, I hadn't expected to have to go undercover here at the hotel this morning.

Mostly because I had no plan at all other than

simply asking what room Alice was staying in, and was caught completely at unawares when I was rejected.

Taking one last look at myself in the mirror, I decided I looked enough like a professional housekeeper and not like the woman who had come in here earlier. I shoved all the cards from my wallet into the pocket of my new uniform, then stuffed my regular clothes into my purse and looked around. Underneath the sinks was a large storage area containing extras of all the bathroom necessities. Thankfully, it was unlocked. I shoved my purse into the back, behind about two hundred rolls of toilet paper, and hoped that no one was going to have a plumbing emergency before I could get back here.

I turned and headed back through the hotel, my heart pounding, hoping I was going to get away with this without being arrested.

Chapter 7

Upon leaving the bathroom, I immediately headed in the same direction as the woman with the uniforms, moving with a confident stride. I figured it was important to look like I knew where I was going. After all, I was no longer playing the role of a rich tourist just lazing about; I was now supposed to be an employee who worked here and knew every inch of this place like the back of my hand.

I eventually reached a door with "staff only" etched across the front, and I passed through it, finding myself in what was obviously a general staff meeting area. Whiteboards and lockers abounded, and in the far end was a sign indicating where the laundry was.

"Hey, you," a woman barked.

My heart leapt in my chest. I looked over to see who had called out. She was five feet tall at most, wearing a sweatsuit embroidered with the hotel logo. She had to be in her fifties and had one of those hardened faces full of lines and wrinkles that you just knew meant she had seen a lot of life.

I pointed at myself with a questioning look on my face, and she nodded. "Of course I mean you. You're Angela, the new hire, right?"

"That's me," I lied automatically.

"Well, you're late."

"Sorry, I had to get my uniform," I said.

The woman waved away my excuse. "Doesn't matter. Don't let it happen again, or you're gone. Clarissa is about to get going, so she'll show you the ropes." The woman pointed to a woman in her mid-thirties. Her short hair was cropped in a pixie cut. She hoisted a box of hotel-sized beauty products onto a cart.

"Thanks. Will do," I said, immediately walking over to Clarissa, who looked up at the sound of my footsteps. "Hi, I'm Angela," I said, holding out a hand, which she shook with a smile. "I've been told that you're going to teach me this job today."

"That's right. It's nice to meet you. I'm Clarissa. This is your first day, huh?"

"It is," I said, hoping against all hope that the real Angela was going to be a no-show. After all, the instant she actually arrived, the whole jig would be up. Hopefully she'd found a better job and just hadn't let the Maui Diamond know she wasn't coming after all.

"Well, let's get going. We're doing the top two floors today. We have to be completely finished by the time clients start coming in at three. The early morning is the more relaxing part of the day, the best time to learn. Checkout isn't until eleven, so most guests are still in their rooms. The head housekeeper on each cart—that's me—has a computer letting them know which guests in their assigned parts of the hotel have already checked out, so we do those rooms first. There's only two so far, so if we're lucky, no one else will check out while we do those two, and then we'll get a little break."

"Cool," I said, nodding for Clarissa to continue.

"After eleven, though, it gets intense. We have to have all the rooms finished by three, which means we have four hours to do a majority of the rooms, since most guests won't leave until they have to, and we also have to do the rooms for guests staying another night. So pay attention early on, because we won't have time for mistakes by the time eleven rolls around."

I nodded, stealing a quick glance at my phone. It was just after nine.

"Now, you grab the other end of the cart, and off we go."

Clarissa led me to the service elevator, which we took up to the fifth floor.

"Our first room for the day is number 515," Clarissa said, looking at the little computer hooked onto her cart.

We headed to the room, and as soon as Clarissa opened the door, I scrunched my nose. There was food *everywhere*. Four slices of pizza were just sitting on the bed, and fat melted into the topsheet. The trash can was filled to the brim with empty beer cans. A half-eaten lollipop was stuck to the pillow. This was disgusting.

Clarissa, however, just walked in as if nothing was wrong.

"Is this normal?" I asked, and she chuckled. "This

isn't even bad. At least it's just food. I once came into a room where the toilet was clogged with condoms."

"You're joking."

"I wish I was."

No wonder the real Angela had decided not to show up for work after all.

Clarissa showed me exactly how to dispose of the junk left everywhere, strip the bed, clean the bathroom, vacuum the floors, and just generally get the hotel room back in tip-top shape for the next person who was going to spend five hundred bucks a night for the privilege of leaving a couple slices of Domino's on the pillow.

"If a guest leaves something behind that's important, put it in here, and we'll take it down to lost and found," Clarissa explained.

I nodded. After we had done the first two rooms, I was starting to get the hang of things, and rather than her explaining to me how to properly fit the sheets on the bed or telling me which cleaner to use for the shower, Clarissa and I began just chatting.

"So where did you grow up?" Clarissa asked.

"On the island. I moved when I was sixteen, though, back to the mainland. You?"

"I moved here three years ago. Came on holiday and never left. It helps that I met the man of my dreams. We're getting married next summer."

"Congratulations," I said.

"Thanks."

"Where's the honeymoon going to be?"

"We were thinking of going to Europe. I've never been."

"Ohhh, that would be nice. I'd love to see Paris one day. And Rome. Those are high on my bucket list. But I also want to go to Australia."

"Australia doesn't really exist, you know," Clarissa said.

I laughed. "What?"

"When it was started as a penal colony all those years ago, the British actually made it up to hide the fact that they were simply murdering the criminals. But then, the idea of it gained so much traction that they couldn't sweep the existence of this Australia under the rug, so they had to keep up the charade. Now, they hire actors to pretend to be Australians so that people still believe the country exists, when it reality it doesn't."

For maybe the first time in my life, I was genuinely completely speechless for a few moments.

"Are you… are you serious?" I eventually asked, hoping that Clarissa just had a real deadpan sense of humor and that I wasn't getting it.

"Of course I'm serious. It's true. Not a lot of people believe it, but that's because they simply automatically believe what they're taught to believe."

"What about pictures taken from space?"

"Photoshopped."

"What about all the people from Australia?"

"As I said, they're actors. Do you know anyone who has actually *been* to Australia?"

"No, I guess I don't," I had to admit. "But that doesn't make it a fake place."

"Look at their animals. What kind of country has

that many poisonous snakes and spiders? And drop bears! Have you heard of drop bears?"

"I haven't," I admitted.

"They fall from trees and kill people. Or so they say. They don't really exist, because Australia doesn't really exist. All this talk of poisonous animals is to discourage people from going, because they don't want people knowing that it's all a ruse."

Cool. My new fake coworker was a straight-up conspiracy theorist. I made a mental note not to bring up 5G or microchips.

"What about kangaroos?"

"They're not real. Look at those things. Do they really look like they should actually exist?"

Okay, she had a point there. "They're weird-looking, but I mean, so are giraffes," I said. "Do you think those are fake, too?"

"Don't be ridiculous. Of course giraffes are real."

Great, now the conspiracy theorist was calling *me* ridiculous.

"Sorry," I said with a laugh, avoiding the urge to roll my eyes. "This is just a lot to take in. What about flights?"

"They're all fake," Clarissa said with complete confidence. "They fly Qantas planes around, but there's never anyone in them. They just go from airport to airport to make people think there are real flights to and from Australia."

"What about people that you know that have gone on holiday there?"

"I don't know any, and neither do you. People who *do* claim to have gone are paid government agents who use Photoshop to get vacation pictures."

Well, if you'd asked me yesterday about the craziest conspiracy theory I'd ever heard, I would have had a different answer than I did now.

"All right," I said. "So Australia is fake."

"You can look it up on the internet," Clarissa said earnestly. "There are lots of people who know the truth, who don't let themselves be controlled by the government and the media and their narrative that Australia is real."

"I will do that."

"Good. It's nice to have a coworker who doesn't instantly write me off as a crazy person when I tell them this. I mean, it's sad, because they're the ones who don't see the truth."

"Yes, the idea that Australia's existence is an elaborate hoax perpetrated and continued by the British government to hide mass murder certainly makes more sense than the idea that it's a normal country that exists."

"Exactly," Clarissa replied, not catching on to the sarcasm in my voice at all.

"Do you think the earth is flat?" I asked.

Clarissa snorted. "Of course not. I'm not an *idiot.*"

"No, I didn't mean to imply you were." Inwardly, my brain was screaming.

"That's a conspiracy theory. This is completely different. This is fact."

"Right. My mistake."

We moved on to the next room, and I made a mental note to never bring up Australia in front of Clarissa again. It shouldn't be too hard, after all, if the continent didn't exist.

Luckily, apart from the weird conspiracy theory, Clarissa was pretty nice. I found out she lived in Kihei as well, in a studio apartment with her fiancé.

We got through all of the rooms, and luckily, none of them had been nearly as disgusting as the first one. Then Clarissa stopped in front of room 522.

"This one's next. The guest is still here, so we always do our best to avoid touching their things. Vacuum around stuff, that sort of thing. If there are clothes on the floor, you can fold them up and place them nicely somewhere if you want, but you don't have to."

"Yeah, I'm not touching weird dirty stranger clothes if I don't have to," I said.

Clarissa laughed. "My attitude exactly. Listen, we're out of toilet paper. Do you mind getting started while I run down and get some more?"

"Sure," I replied.

Clarissa knocked on the door. "Housekeeping!"

There was no reply, so she nodded and looked at me.

"I'll just open the door for you. I'll see you in a minute," Clarissa said, pressing her master key against the black pad on the door. A green light appeared as there came a click from the lock coming undone, and I pressed down on the handle while Clarissa headed down the hall.

I pushed my cart into the room and could immediately sense something was wrong. There was someone in this room, and they were hiding from me.

Chapter 8

My instinct was to get out of the room immediately. I could *sense* the presence of someone here, but I didn't know why they wouldn't just show themselves. Whose room was this, anyway? Besides, if I shouted for Clarissa to come back because I thought something was wrong, but there was nothing, I'd be considered the crazy one.

Then again, what did I care? It wasn't like I was really this Angela person. I was just trying to figure out what room was Alice Doherty's so I could come back later and speak with her. I could just leave and avoid the serial killer who was probably hiding in the closet.

"Housekeeping," I called out again cautiously. Maybe I was wrong. Maybe there was no one here.

That was when my eyes landed on the sheet of paper on the floor. The letterhead read *Kinolio Resort*, and it was addressed to Alice Doherty. This was it. I was in her room.

Was someone in here waiting for her to come back so they could kill her too?

I grabbed a bottle of the most toxic bathroom cleaner we had and held it in front of me with my finger on the spray trigger as I looked around the room. It was huge, no doubt about that. I had entered a living room with the bathroom to my left and a huge couch and flat-screen TV directly in front of me. There was nowhere there where a person could hide, so I peeked into the bathroom. It was practically the size of my old apartment in Seattle, complete with spa bathtub, a huge walk-in shower, double vanities, and a toilet in its own separate room.

Nowhere for a serial killer to hide, though. If there was someone here with me, they were in the bedroom.

I passed through the sliding double doors and into the bedroom, doing my best James Bond impression with the spray as I looked for the intruder. Again, huge: a king-sized bed in the middle of the room, another wall-mounted TV, a full desk with a laptop sitting on it, and a set of closets near the back of the room. The closets were the perfect place to hide.

My heart pounded so hard in my chest I was sure whoever was in there would hear me coming a mile away, but luckily, the plush carpet beneath my feet hid the sound of my shoes.

I crept up toward the closet, took a deep—and silent—breath, and opened the door.

As soon as I did, someone jumped out and shoved me. I reacted without thinking and squirted the bathroom cleaner into my attacker's face as fast as I could.

"What the hell?" the attacker screamed.

That gave me enough time to scramble out of the way and get a look at who it was. When I realized I knew her, I gasped. "You're that old lady from the coffee shop!"

"Who are you calling old?" Dorothy asked, her hands on her hips. "And what did you spray on me? You could have at least made it vodka."

"You! You're at least seventy. That makes you old by literally anyone's definition."

"You watch your mouth, young lady."

"Whatever. You can't be in here. I'm calling security."

"Oh, please, like you actually work here. I don't believe that for a second. You're here to try and sneak information from Alice Doherty."

"So are you!" I retorted.

"Now, ladies," the other old lady, Rosie, said suddenly. She was squeezing herself out from underneath the bed, and I had to admit I was impressed at the fact that she'd gotten herself under there. It looked like there had to be less than a foot of space. Getting to her feet with an agility and grace I never would have expected for a woman of her age, she looked at the two of us.

I still held the bathroom cleaner in front of me, while globs of it dripped down the side of Dorothy's face.

"Look. This is ridiculous. We can't keep bumping into each other like this, and at the same time, we're obviously the three people who are closest to solving this murder. What do you say we all join forces?"

I looked at Rosie skeptically, while Dorothy shook her head emphatically.

"Not a chance," she said. "I want my share of that hundred grand, and that share is fifty percent. I'm not going down to thirty-three just because some kid thinks she's going to get there before us."

"Thirty-three is still better than zero if she does get there," Rosie pointed out. "Besides, she's obviously capable. She's managed to get into this room on her wits alone. The three of us working together would be able to solve this faster. What do you say?"

Rosie turned to me, and I considered her words. She had a point, actually. The two old ladies always seemed to be one step ahead of me. Maybe joining forces with them wasn't a bad idea.

"Okay," I said, nodding. "I'm in if you are. But decide quickly. My coworker is coming back in a minute, and if she finds you here, she's going to call security for real, because unlike me, she actually does work here."

Dorothy frowned and looked at Rosie. "You're sure this is a good idea?"

"I am," Rosie said.

"All right, I trust your instincts. Let's do it."

"Okay," I said quickly. "I'm going to have to actually clean this room, but I'll see what I can find out while I do. The two of you go into the bathroom. I'll tell Clarissa I've already cleaned it. That way she won't go in, but hide in the shower just in case. I'm finished working at four. Meet me in the lobby at, say, four fifteen, and we'll go over what we've got so far. And maybe get to talk with Alice."

Rosie nodded. "Got it. We'll see you then."

"Do you really trust her? She shot me with bathroom cleaner," Dorothy complained.

"Come on, Dot," Rosie said, grabbing her friend by the arm and dragging her toward the bathroom.

A moment later, Clarissa returned with a giant pack of toilet paper.

"Perfect, you got it," I said. "Let me grab a roll off you. I've finished cleaning the bathroom otherwise." I hoped Alice Doherty wasn't the type to complain to management that her bathroom hadn't been cleaned to the hotel's exacting standards today.

I snuck into the bathroom, quickly changed the roll of toilet paper, then headed back out. "I did the whole bathroom, but the rest of the room needs to be done."

"Great," Clarissa said, and the two of us set about cleaning. I grabbed the sheet of paper I'd found on the floor and sneakily took a picture of it with my phone while Clarissa vacuumed. Hopefully it would have some information that might lead to her boss's killer.

I scanned the room for more information that might help us as I cleaned, but it was unfortunately bare in that respect. The laptop was locked on the home screen, and it wasn't as though I'd be able to have a good look at it anyway with Clarissa here. Hopefully, when we left, Rosie and Dorothy would have better luck than me.

I was on tenterhooks the entire time as we cleaned the room. At any minute, I expected Clarissa to want to check on my work in the bathroom or come up with some other reason to be in there, but she didn't, and as soon as we left and headed down the hall to the next room, I breathed a sigh of relief.

I only had to get through a few more rooms; then I'd be meeting Rosie and Dorothy in the lobby and hopefully be well on my way to finding James MacMahon's killer.

By four o'clock, my feet hurt and I was starting to get grumpy. After all, I wasn't really Angela, so I wasn't even getting paid to spend my day off cleaning what seemed like half this hotel, even though it was only one floor.

"I'll see you tomorrow," Clarissa said to me when we were finished, giving me a wave.

"Sure will," I lied. A part of me wanted to leave a note in Clarissa's locker, telling her I was from the Australian government, and that we were going to send robot kangaroos after her, but I figured that was probably tempting fate a little bit too much. Besides, I didn't know exactly which locker was Clarissa's. Oh well.

I headed back out the way I had come and went back to the bathroom where I had stashed my things. Thankfully, my purse was still there, and five minutes later, I was myself once more. I folded the uniform I'd used and left it on a nearby stool—I wasn't about to take it home with me—and walked back out to the lobby.

Rosie and Dorothy were sitting on a set of comfortable-looking wicker chairs. Rosie was busy knitting away, acting like the stereotypical older woman, seemingly completely innocent, giving no indication to passersby that she had recently broken into someone's hotel room and searched it while looking for a murderer.

Dorothy, sitting next to her, was busy reading a book. I glanced at the title: *How to Murder People Who Interrupt You When You're Reading.*

My laugh caused them both to look up, and Dorothy scowled. "Here I thought you were reneging on our deal."

I checked my phone. It was almost four thirty.

"Damn, I didn't realize we worked late. Sorry."

"Well, you're here now, and that's what's important. I'm Rosie," the other woman said, holding out a hand.

"Charlotte," I replied, shaking it. "But you can call me Charlie. Everyone else does."

"It's nice to meet you, Charlie," Rosie said. "This is Dorothy."

"If I'm calling you Charlie, you may as well call me Dot."

"I have to ask, is that really the title of the book you're reading?" I asked, motioning to the cover.

She removed it and laughed. "No. I've printed off a few of these to slip over hardbacks. It usually garners a few laughs, and that way, most people are afraid to ask me what I'm actually reading, which is the whole point."

"Fair enough," I said. "So, what did the two of you find out in Alice's room?"

"She spends ninety percent of her paycheck on underwear," Dot replied immediately, and Rosie scowled at her.

"That's not what she means. We did manage to have a quick look through her laptop."

"I installed some spyware on it, too, so we can access it remotely," Dot said, suddenly turning serious. "We should go to my house, where we can check it out. If she knows anything, it'll be there."

I nodded. "I want to talk to her, but I think I'll wait until tomorrow, lest I be recognized, seeing as I don't actually work here."

"I figured," Rosie replied with a small smile. "You'll have to tell us how you managed to fake your way into a maid's role for a day."

"Only if you tell me how you actually got into her room."

"Deal."

The three of us got up and left the hotel, and I followed the two old ladies in their car to a small apartment complex about half a mile from my mom's place. Low-rise brick, and obviously built in the sixties, the complex was old but nicely cared for, with a cute, manicured garden at the front and freshly resurfaced pavement in the parking area.

I slid Mom's car into a visitor's spot and walked over to the ten-year-old Honda SUV Rosie drove.

"This is where Dot lives," Rosie explained, motioning at the building.

"And don't you tell anyone," she warned, wagging a finger in my face.

I legitimately wasn't sure if she was kidding.

"So, what do you know so far?" Rosie asked.

"I know James MacMahon was in a taxi headed to the airport when he was killed," I said. "I spoke to the cab driver. MacMahon got a text, asked the driver to pull over, got out, went behind the building, and next thing anyone knew, he was dead."

"What was your read on the cab driver?" Rosie asked. "Think he was the one who did it?"

I shook my head. "No motive. I mean, I know a ton of people hated the Kinolio Resort, but would you really recognize the guy in charge of it on sight?"

"I suppose it depends," Rosie mused. "If the taxi driver was Charles, for example, I'm sure he knew who the person in charge was."

"True. A crime of opportunity, then? But what kind of taxi driver keeps a knife ready and waiting in case he happens upon a customer who would be good to stab? And how would he have lured James MacMahon behind that building? If a taxi driver stops and asks me to get out of his cab and follow him, you can bet your ass I'd be jumping out of that car the next chance I got."

"Good point," Dot said. "I agree. If the cab driver had anything, it would have been a gun. And he probably wouldn't have called the cops to report a crime he committed; he would have bailed out of there as fast as he could."

"Okay, so it likely wasn't him," Rosie said as we stopped in front of the door to apartment number 23. Dot pressed her phone against a keypad, and the deadbolt whirred open. I raised my eyebrows.

"Bluetooth-enabled lock?"

"It's not exactly Bluetooth, but yes. It's more secure than just using a traditional key." Dorothy replied. "I have to have my phone unlocked before it'll work, and since I use facial recognition to unlock it, it would be almost impossible for someone to get in that way. They'd have to be extremely skilled to get through this lock. You can't hack it as easily as a regular Bluetooth connection."

I raised my eyebrows. I was actually pretty impressed at how adept with technology Dot appeared to be.

When we walked into the apartment, my mouth dropped open. I had expected standard old-lady fare, to be honest—floral motif couches, kitschy decorations on the shelves, an old CRT television that looked like it hadn't been turned on in about a decade… instead, I found myself in the middle of a modern technological haven.

A huge flat-screen TV filled the living room, with built-in speakers hung around for a full surround-sound experience. At a desk on the left-hand side of the room was a computer setup with four monitors, a gaming chair, and an ergonomic keyboard.

The kitchen looked practically abandoned, and Dot appeared to live entirely off takeout food and granola bars.

The only sign that the occupant of this place wasn't a twenty-two-year-old boy with his daddy's credit card was the bookcase to the left of the entryway, filled top to bottom with women's fiction. I spotted psychological thrillers—*The Woman on the Train, Gone Girl*, and *Stolen Child*, among others—virtually every Agatha Christie novel known to man, a handful of Liane Moriarty titles, and at the bottom, a handful of nonfiction books on all sorts of technology.

"You like to read?"

Dot nodded. "I was a school librarian for thirty-seven years," she said. "I enjoy my books."

"And this?" I asked, motioning to the computer. "You're obviously good with computers."

"You could say that," Dot said enigmatically, heading toward the desk. She turned on the computer, while Rosie went to the kitchen and helped herself to a glass of water. She motioned to me, silently asking if I wanted one, but I shook my head no.

"What have the two of you found out, then?" I asked.

"Well, James MacMahon is the president and primary shareholder of the company building the Kinolio Resort," Rosie said. "I assume you knew that as well." I nodded, and she continued. "Obviously, there's significant opposition to the deal on Maui."

"That's what happens when you have to bribe county representatives to allow your resort to be built on parkland," Dot muttered from her spot at the computer, and I smiled.

"So you don't actually believe what you said to Charles this morning at Starbucks?"

"Of course not. I just wanted to see what kind of temper he had. His posts on Facebook gave the impression he wasn't particularly stable, and the events yesterday morning proved it."

"I also looked at his posts," I replied. "And found out he worked at the grocery store then just waited for him to come out in the morning."

Rosie nodded approvingly. "See? This is why we

brought you on board. The three of us seem to be the only ones actually doing this properly. We still think he's a prime suspect."

"Me too," I replied. "After all, he obviously had a temper, and he practically strangled Dot in front of us. I'm not sure what would have happened if I hadn't hit him with the chair."

"Nothing a kick to the nuts wouldn't have fixed," Dot said casually as she tapped away at her keyboard.

"There's only one problem," I said. "I don't know how Charles would have gotten a hold of James's phone number and what he would have texted to get him to stop a cab on the way to the airport. It had to be very important, because James was in a huge rush. He was stressed about something."

"How do you know?"

"I'm the one who called the cab for him. His Uber account got hacked, and he didn't know the number for the cab company, so he came in to ask for it. While he was waiting for it to show up, we spoke a little bit, and I heard him on the phone. He was stressed and upset about his flights back to the mainland, but I wonder if it was more than that. I wonder if it had anything to do with his lunch."

"Oh?" Rosie asked. "We don't know anything about him having lunch."

I nodded and filled them in on what I'd found out about his meal with Calvin Monroe.

"Well, it sounds like we have another suspect on our list."

"Exactly. And not only would this one have known

James's phone number, but James probably would have stopped to meet him if Calvin told him it was an emergency."

"Right," Rosie replied, nodding.

"All right, if the two of you want to come over here, Alice is using her computer," Dot said. "We can see everything she's doing in real time."

Rosie and I immediately scurried over to see what the murder victim's assistant was looking at.

Chapter 9

"How did you do this?" I asked Dot, impressed.

"Spyware installed on her laptop when we were in her room," Dot answered as if it were the most natural thing in the world. "This is a really good program, too. She won't notice the computer's slowed down at all."

"Can it be tracked back to here?"

The withering look Dorothy gave me in reply was obviously a no. "Do you think I'm an amateur?"

"Seeing as you just told me you spent three decades working as a librarian, then yeah, unless your side hustle involved being a hacker for the CIA."

"I may never have done this as a job, but I am no amateur," Dot replied. "I was using ARPANET before you were born."

"Ladies, ladies," Rosie interrupted. "Can we please swing our ovaries around later? What's Alice looking at?"

The three of us moved our focus to the computer, where Alice had just opened up her e-mail account.

It was strange to watch the screen as the mouse moved along by itself. "We can't control her screen, can we?" I asked Dot.

She shook her head. "No. I didn't have time to implant something like that on her computer. We wanted to be in and out in under ten minutes once we saw her go down to lunch. Besides, we don't want to alert her to the fact that we're watching."

Alice had just opened an email from Hawaiian Airlines. She was flying back to New York City four days from now, leaving on the afternoon flight to LA before connecting back to the East Coast.

"I guess her extra time here in Hawaii is over," I mused. "Maybe they're done with the autopsy."

"It wouldn't surprise me if they pushed it to the front of the line," Rosie said. "After all, as far as I know, Maui County hasn't had any other murders recently, and I doubt Honolulu's morgue is stacked with bodies, either."

"Plus, a man like that, they're going to want to solve it. Business tourist with enough money to buy half the island? There's going to be a lot of pressure to put someone in jail," Dot added.

I nodded in agreement.

"What it does mean is we only have a few more days to talk to her," Rosie said.

"We should go back to the hotel tonight," I suggested. "It's not late yet."

"Hold on. Look at this," Dot said. Alice had clicked

off from the email with her flight details and had opened one from someone named Bernard. Going by the email address, he worked for the same company as James MacMahon. Alice scrolled through the email and began typing a reply, giving the three of us enough time to read what Bernard had sent her.

Thank you for staying in Hawaii until the arrangements are made. I'm in contact with the district attorney in Maui, as well as the coroner in Honolulu. In a few days, everything should be arranged, at which point it should be fine for you to come back to New York. I'll have my assistant book your flight back over and email you the confirmation. I know this must have been a traumatic time for you, and I want you to know I've organized for a grief counsellor to come into the office. Given your close working relationship with James, I've organized for you to have some private sessions with her as well. Please let me know if there's anything I can do.

Bernard Jones

Alice was replying to the email even as I read.

Thank you, Bernard, for the kind words and the offer. As beautiful as Hawaii is, I'm looking forward to coming home. I can't help but shudder every time I think of James and what happened to him, and I haven't left the hotel since I heard the news, except to meet with the detectives in charge of the case. I'll be happy when I'm back in New York.

Alice

"We have three days to speak to her," Dot said. "Why don't we do it tomorrow? It sounds like she's not leaving the hotel, so we could grab breakfast there and just so happen to run into her."

I shook my head. "I can't. I have to work. Today was my day off."

"Well, dinner then. There was no sign that she was ordering room service, so she must be eating at one of the hotel restaurants."

I nodded. "I could do dinner. I'll have to borrow a bit of money from a friend of mine, but yeah, it should be fine."

Dot shot me a look. "Do you seriously not have a career that allows you to have even one dinner out?"

"Well, maybe if your generation hadn't completely trashed the economy, I'd be doing a lot better."

"Somehow, I feel like the overall status of the economy is not the only problem here."

"Are you saying I don't seem to have my life together?" I asked, crossing my arms. I was offended, despite the fact that it was entirely the truth. My life status was currently "Jenga tower that a kitten on cocaine had jumped directly into the center of."

"You're wearing a shirt with an ice cream stain on it, your socks don't match, and you just spent an entire day doing housekeeping for a hotel you don't work for," Dorothy replied.

"Yeah, well, nyah nyah nyah," I muttered in reply, casually looking around for the ice cream stain. Damn, there it was, on the hem of my shirt on the left-hand side. I hadn't even noticed it.

"All right, well, in the interest of the two of you actually getting along, I'll buy dinner tomorrow night," Rosie offered.

"Score, we got her," Dot said, offering me a high five.

I laughed and shook my head while slapping her hand back. I didn't quite get her, but she seemed fun. She certainly didn't act like any other old lady that I knew. I had never met a septuagenarian hacker before—although, to be fair, I'd never actually met any hackers, period.

Rosie shook her head. "You're impossible, Dot. Anyway, that's the plan for tomorrow. Should we do anything else tonight?"

"I want to check out the crime scene," I answered. "The cops should be finished with it by now. But you never know what they missed."

"Very good thinking," Dot agreed. "Let's see if we can find anything there the cops missed as soon as Alice leaves her computer."

The three of us kept our eyes glued to the screen for a few minutes, but it didn't take long before Alice closed all the programs she'd opened and then the screen went black.

"I guess that's it for the night for her," I said with a shrug.

"Right," Dorothy said, jumping up from the chair. "Let's go check out the crime scene."

WE DECIDED TO WALK, SINCE DOROTHY'S APARTMENT was only a few minutes away from where the murder had taken place. Even at night, even in October, Maui was warm enough to wander around in a T-shirt, and a warm breeze tickled my bare arms as the warm glow from the streetlights shone down on us.

"So, I know Dot was a librarian. What did you do before you retired?" I asked Rosie.

"I worked as a teller at the bank my whole adult life," Rosie replied. "I retired at sixty-five. Working at the bank taught me everything I needed to know about investments."

"Are you as good with computers as Dorothy?" I asked.

Rosie shook her head. "Goodness, no. We're not even in the same galaxy in that respect. I can get around on the internet, and I have an email account, but that's about it. In fact, it was when the bank decided to move to those new-fangled fancy computers with programs to do everything that I decided my time had long since come and gone, and I retired."

"How about you? Why did you move to the island?" Dot asked.

"A family of drug dealers in Seattle was trying to kill me," I replied. "Their low-life brother robbed the jewelry store I was working at, he ended up dead, and they blame me."

"Well, that's quite the story," Rosie said, obviously surprised.

"Believe me, I'd rather be in Seattle right now, not knowing what a severed finger looked like," I replied.

"Some people just find adventure wherever they go," Dot said. "Better to embrace it. Too many people lead boring lives. They grow up, they have a career, they have kids, they get sick, and they die without ever having anything interesting happen to them."

"Spoken like someone who's never had to shoot someone who was trying to kill them."

"Wow," Rosie said. "You shot one of them?"

"I didn't have a choice. Believe me, I'd would much rather it had gone differently."

We reached the spot where James MacMahon had been killed a moment later. Sure enough, all sign of police presence had completely disappeared. Gone was the yellow tape; gone were the red-and-blue lights; gone were the investigators.

I pointed out the parking lot where the cabbie had been parked and the building behind which the body had been found.

"We'll check that out, first," Rosie said, taking charge and leading the way.

I pulled out my phone, turning on the flashlight to get a better look at the ground, and Dot did the same. Rosie struggled with hers for a minute, but Dot eventually went over and turned the app on for her. "I always told you that you needed me to see the light," she joked, and Rosie rolled her eyes.

"What are we looking for?" I asked.

"Anything that looks like it could possibly have been used in the murder," Rosie said. "Start where the body was, and move outward. It could be something as simple as a discarded cigarette butt."

"Shouldn't the cops have found anything that might be useful?"

"You never know what they missed. Besides, while

some of the cops on this island are decent and know what they're doing, a lot… are not," Dot said.

I nodded. That had been the case back when I lived on the island as well. Not that we'd had a lot of run-ins with the cops. But it was well known that some of them were much better at their jobs than others.

"This is where the body was, as best as I can remember," I said, motioning to the spot where I'd seen James MacMahon's body, the knife sticking out of him. "He had been stabbed."

"Do you remember what kind of knife it was?" Rosie asked. "Anything you can think of to describe it. You never know; it might be important."

I closed my eyes, trying to think back. "Unfortunately, I was mostly focused on the blood and the fact that he was dead," I said slowly as I racked my brain. "The knife was small. It wasn't a chef's knife or anything like that. I could only see the handle, obviously. It was light in color, and it shone a bit in the light, like it had a glossy handle, but that's all I remember."

"Okay," Rosie said. "But it wasn't a hunting knife or a Swiss Army knife or anything like that?"

I thought back. "No, I'm pretty sure it wasn't."

"What are you thinking?" Dot asked.

"If the knife was something that a person wouldn't ordinarily carry, then it means they would have had to bring it here on purpose."

"Meaning you're thinking it was premeditated murder and not just a spur-of-the-moment thing," I finished, nodding slowly.

"Exactly," Rosie said. "That can certainly impact

both the motive and the mentality the killer might have had."

"It's a point in Charles's favor," I pointed out. "Not only would he have no real way of knowing James MacMahon's phone number, but James would have no reason to stop for him, *and* he doesn't strike me as the sort of guy who premeditates his dinner for the night, let alone a murder."

"I agree," Dot said. "Charles might have anger issues, and he's *way* too obsessed with this new development, but I can't see him as a premeditated killer."

I nodded. "Okay. Let's split up. Meet back here in a few minutes. If you see something, call out."

We each chose a direction in which to search. I headed away from the building and toward the trees at the far end of the lot. I scanned the ground carefully, the beam of my flashlight forcing me to focus on the ground only a few inches at a time, which was perfect. I stared intently, looking for anything that might betray the killer.

Unfortunately, as time passed, I moved farther and farther away from the crime scene and still didn't have anything that could remotely be considered evidence. I was starting to lose faith that we were going to find anything. I had just about reached the end of the park when I heard Dorothy call out.

"Hey, I think I've got something!"

I perked up at this and immediately headed over to where Dorothy stood.

She was against the wall of the building blocking the murder scene from view of the road. "Look, just there," she said, pointing her light at a piece of rock from which there hung a tiny string of thread.

"What color is that?" Rosie asked, squinting.

"Blue, either navy or cobalt," I replied. "It's in the darker family of blues."

"Right," Dot said. "I bet it belongs to our killer. I bet he laid in wait here, leaning against the building, for James MacMahon to show up, and this got snagged on a piece of jagged brick."

"It's possible," I said. "But what if it was just some kid playing baseball who ran over and smacked himself into the wall while grabbing the ball from the ground?"

"Maybe," Dot admitted. "But it's unlikely. Given more than a couple of days, this string would have fallen off the brick. There hasn't been anyone here the last day or so, what with it being a crime scene and all, so I think this came from the killer, and the cops missed it."

"So whoever killed James MacMahon had been wearing blue," Rosie mused.

Dot nodded. "It's not much, but it's *something*."

"You're right, it's not much," I muttered, feeling a tad deflated. But then, what had I been hoping for? That the police would have come by and missed a glaring piece of evidence, like the murder weapon, and just left it lying on the grass?

"Did either one of you find anything else?" Dot asked.

Both Rosie and I shook our heads no. "This is the best we've got, I think," I said.

"I think we're best off calling it a night here," Rosie added. "Tomorrow, we'll have dinner at the Maui

Diamond, and hopefully we'll get a chance to speak with Alice."

I had just opened my mouth to agree when an authoritative male voice suddenly sounded behind me.

"Police. Stop right there."

Chapter 10

I froze, my heart leaping into my throat. *The cops.*

"This is a crime scene. What are you doing here?"

The officer shined a flashlight directly into my face, and I raised my hand to shield my eyes from the glare.

"Officers, good evening," Rosie said, calm as anything. "What can we do for two of Maui's finest?"

"You can tell me what you're doing here," the man grunted.

As the beam of his flashlight moved away and my eyes got used to the light, I finally got my first decent look at the cops. There were two of them, both male. Neither one of them was in uniform, but one held up a badge. The one who had been speaking to us was older, maybe in his mid-fifties, with a decent-sized beer belly and creases all over his face that made him look older than he probably was. He looked like the kind of man who frowned a lot. His shirt wasn't tucked into his wrinkled slacks, and I was fairly certain there were sprinkles of icing sugar across his chest.

His partner, on the other hand, the one with the badge… wow. He was at least six feet tall, and his muscles strained against his fitted polo shirt, incapable of hiding just how much time this guy must have spent at the gym. His black slacks were spotless, his face tinted with just a bit of stubble that enhanced the cut of his cheekbones. His deep brown hair had that ruffled, just-got-out-of-bed look, and the color contrasted with his blue eyes beautifully.

I'd let him handcuff me any day…

Rosie answered, and I snapped back to reality. "Why hello, officers. We're just a couple of women enjoying the park on this fine night."

"That's detective to you. You are aware this is a crime scene, right?" the older man said gruffly.

"Well, it might have been in the past, but I don't see any signs or tape cordoning this place off," Dot replied, looking around innocently. "I thought that meant we were free to come here. Awful, what happened to that poor man. Just awful."

"You wouldn't be here looking for clues in the hopes of getting that reward money, would you?" the police detective spat. "I can't believe they offered that. Now we get random strangers trampling through the crime scene at all hours."

"Us? No, of course not. We're just three women heading to the beach tonight."

"Well, we got a call from someone claiming to have seen some suspicious lights around here."

"That may have been us, but don't worry, detectives. We weren't doing anything wrong, just trying to get to the beach" Rosie insisted.

"Have you been drinking?"

"Come on, Liam," the younger cop said. "These women are obviously not causing any trouble. Why don't we all just agree to go on our merry way?" He flashed me a smile, and I swear I melted into a pool of goo right then and there. It had been *way* too long since I had been with a man.

"No. I've had it with these people who see the reward money and think they can go around and play cops. They have no training, they have no idea what they're doing, and they think they're going to find something here? I want to see some ID from all three of you ladies."

Unable to help myself, I rolled my eyes as I reached into my purse to grab my driver's license.

"Was that an eyeroll?" Liam shot at me, spittle shooting from his mouth and onto my face.

I grimaced and wiped it away with my sleeve. I didn't like cops like this. He was obviously one of those power-hungry jackasses who didn't care about actually protecting anyone and just enjoyed being able to carry a gun around and intimidate people.

"I'm sure it wasn't," the other officer said, obviously trying to defuse the situation.

"Stay out of this, Jake," Liam snarled in reply. "That's insubordination, and it's assaulting a police officer."

"Oh, please," I shot back, my mouth taking over.

"The only thing assaulting anyone here is your stomach against that belt."

Dot started coughing in an attempt to hide the fact that she'd burst out laughing, and it didn't work at all.

"That's it. You bitches are all under arrest," Liam snarled.

"Hey, hey, there's no need for any of this," Jake said, stepping between me and Liam, but Liam shoved Jake to the side.

"No, enough is enough. I'm bringing them in."

"On what charge?" Rosie asked, standing tall and staring Liam down. Even though she was a solid foot shorter than him, Rosie had an authority about her right now that made her appear quite a bit bigger than she was. I was impressed. Hopefully when I was in my seventies, I would be just as badass as her.

"This is harassment," Dot scowled. "We're just three women in a public park, and you two cops come at us like we're breaking the law. Meanwhile, you let the actual perverts hanging around go free."

"That's it," Liam said again, grabbing a pair of cuffs from his belt. "I'm taking these ladies in."

"Like hell you are," Dot said, grabbing the cuffs from his hands and throwing them up onto the roof of the building, where they landed with a clatter, well out of reach of any of us.

My mouth dropped open, shocked. I mean, I had a mouth that could get me into trouble. Heck, it had gotten me into trouble more times than I was proud to admit. But grabbing a cop's handcuffs as he was about to arrest me and throwing them where no one could get them? Dot had just taken things to a whole new level.

"All right, that's enough," Jake said, pulling out his own cuffs.

Before he got a chance to do anything with them, though, Liam pulled a Taser from his belt.

"No!" I shouted, springing into action before I could consider whether what I was doing was a good idea.

I mean, Dot was in her seventies, at least. Being Tased could kill her. So I immediately jumped forward and knocked Liam's arm out of the way, and the next thing I knew, my entire body convulsed with pain.

And then everything went black.

I WOKE UP WITH A SPLITTING HEADACHE, THE SOUND of a heart rate monitor beeping rhythmically every few seconds. My mouth was dry, my muscles felt like I'd spent the entire day at the gym, and I was just generally very, very sore.

I groaned and tried to move over but heard a clink. I looked down to see that I was handcuffed to the bed, and everything started coming back to me.

"Are you shitting me?" I called out to no one in particular.

"Welcome back to the world," a voice beside me said.

I turned to find myself staring into the gorgeous blue eyes of that younger cop, the one who had tried to defuse the situation. Jake—that was his name.

I narrowed my eyes at him and wiggled the cuffed arm. "What, did you think while I was unconscious, I was going to run off?"

Jake shrugged. "I don't make the rules. I just follow them."

"If only your partner followed them, too. What was he thinking, trying to Taser an old lady like that? Is Dot okay?"

"Dorothy and Rosie are fine," Jake replied. "Calm down."

"I will *not* calm down," I snapped. As the memory of what had happened began coming back to me, I just got angrier. That cop had really tried to Taser Dorothy. "Why the hell am I in handcuffs, anyway? I'm the one who got Tased."

"I'm working on sorting that out," Jake said. "Don't worry. I don't think you're going to get charged."

"I bloody better not get charged unless you want the entire media to hear the story of how an out-of-control power freak on a bender decided to Taser a woman in her seventies for *daring* to be in a public park at night, minding her own business."

I knew I sounded hysterical, but I didn't care.

"You tell him, sister!" Dorothy shouted from outside the room.

I looked smugly at Jake, who just looked exhausted. "Let them come in here."

"I can't do that."

"Why are you in here, then?"

"You're under arrest, and you need to be supervised

by a police officer until you can be processed. That's protocol."

"And what part of protocol includes using a Taser on people simply enjoying themselves in the park?"

Jake sighed. "I'm not a fan of what happened back there, off the record."

"Why aren't you dressed like a cop, anyway? You're detectives, right? There's no way you'd have been called out for people being in the park at night."

"Liam and I are the lead detectives in the James MacMahon murder," Jake replied. "As a result, we're the ones getting called whenever people traipse all over our crime scene."

"Have you possibly considered not Tasering them? And also using normal-people words like 'walked' instead of 'traipse'?"

A smile fluttered on Jake's lips. "If you hadn't done your best Refrigerator Perry impression and tried to take out my partner, maybe you wouldn't have been Tased."

"Better me than Dorothy. He could have given her a heart attack."

"Yeah," he replied, obviously not pleased. "Trust me, nothing about tonight went the way I wanted it to."

"So why was he so aggressive toward us, anyway? Does he just get off on abusing innocent people?"

"We've been inundated with calls since the reward was made public," Jake offered with a shrug of his shoulders. "It's hard enough working a murder investigation at the best of times. But when you've got half the island thinking they're going to help, when they're actually only in the way, it gets frustrating."

"I work at an ice cream store, and sometimes customers try fifteen flavors of ice cream before they settle on the one they want, when there are ten people in line waiting to be served. That's frustrating too, but I don't get to Taser them for it," I replied.

Jake laughed. "You are something, you know that? Look, let me talk to Liam. I'll convince him that it's in his best interest not to press charges."

"Can you undo this in the meantime?" I asked, holding up the handcuffs. "I need to pee, and believe me, if I don't get to freely use the bathroom, I *will* make sure you regret that decision."

Jake pursed his lips for a moment, considering my words. "You're not going to run out of here, are you?"

"Have you ever been Tased? My legs feel like I just ran a marathon. If I tried to make a run for it, the guy down the hall with two broken legs could probably catch me."

"There's a guy down the hall with two broken legs?"

"It was an example, *obviously*," I replied, exasperated. "Now, are you going to let me out of these or not?"

"Not right now. Let me go talk to Liam. I'll be back in a few minutes. I'll see if I can convince him to drop the charges completely."

I fumed in my bed, trying to cross my arms and yanking on the cuffs again. I let out a yelp, and Jake just shook his head as he left the room. I flipped him off as he left. How could someone so hot also be so annoying? I hoped he was successful in getting the charges dropped.

I wanted to move out of my Mom's house, but a jail cell wasn't exactly the new home I had in mind.

A moment later, the door to the room opened again, and Zoe came in. She looked so smart, wearing black dress pants and a button-down sky-blue shirt that looked beautiful against her copper skin. The lab coat over the whole ensemble gave her an extra air of authority, and the stethoscope around her neck screamed, "In case the rest of this outfit didn't make it obvious, I'm a doctor."

"Damn, you dress up nice," I said to her with a grin.

She looked me up and down. "I wish I could say the same about you. I suppose I should congratulate you for making it three full days on the island before ending up in the hospital."

"Hey, I didn't *ask* to be Tased."

"And yet ninety-nine percent of the world population manages to go their entire life without knowing what that feels like. Why am I not surprised you're part of the one percent?"

"When you talk about me being part of the one percent, I wish it was in a different context."

"Me too, trust me. At least you got a private room due to the extra security. Seriously though, how are you feeling?"

"Like a personal trainer who belongs in the depths of hell just put me through a ten-hour workout," I replied. "Every muscle in my body is sore."

Zoe nodded. "Okay, that's pretty normal. It'll pass. Your vitals are fine. I ordered an ECG to check your heart just in case, but I don't think there's any permanent damage. Technically, I could have discharged you an hour ago, but I figured seeing as they're just going to haul you off to jail, I put in a requisition to have you held for observation overnight. After that, I'm not going to have any more medical reasons to keep you here."

"Thanks," I said, shooting Zoe a grateful smile. "I really appreciate it."

"It's the least I can do. I have a sneaking suspicion it's not the last time I'm going to see you here."

"I was saving an old lady's life."

"So I heard," Zoe said, a smile on her lips. "She's your biggest fan now, too. As soon as you came in, she harassed me, making me promise I was going to take care of you like you were my sister."

"You are my sister," I said, reaching over and squeezing Zoe's hand.

She smiled. "I am. And I'm glad you're okay."

"If you see the cop that did this, kick him in the balls for me, okay?"

"You know, I'm starting to understand how you ended up handcuffed in this hospital bed."

"Hey, he deserves it."

"I'm not saying he doesn't," Zoe laughed. "Listen, if you're not in jail by tomorrow afternoon, grab a coffee with me and tell me all about it. I have to keep doing my rounds, but I want to hear this whole story from your mouth as well."

"I will."

Zoe turned to leave, then paused. "And if you do find yourself in jail, call my mom. She's still at the same number as she's always been. She'll get you out."

"Thanks," I said quietly. Zoe's mom had been one

of the best criminal lawyers on the island when we were growing up. Hawaiian born and raised, she had always wanted to fight for the underdog, and that had driven her to become a lawyer. When Zoe's dad, a naval officer stationed on Oahu, had gotten himself in trouble one night, he'd hired Zoe's mom to represent him. Not only did she prove his innocence and ensure that there were no repercussions from the armed forces, but the two of them fell in love. Zoe's dad had retired from the Navy, and the two of them moved to Maui, where Zoe's mom had grown up. The rest was history.

Her mom was partly retired now and only took on cases that especially sparked her interest, and I was humbled to know that even after all these years, she would represent me if it came to that.

"The one cop is trying to convince the other not to press charges," I said, managing a small smile. "Hopefully he's successful."

"I hope so," Zoe replied. "I'll talk to you tomorrow. Do what you can not to get charged, okay?"

"Everyone seems to forget I'm the one who got Tased," I muttered.

"Don't worry. I'm never going to let you forget it, either," Zoe said to me with a wink as she left.

I laughed, my spirits much higher after the visit from my friend. I wasn't sure if she would have normally been assigned to me or if she had specifically asked to treat me. But either way, I was grateful.

Now I just had to hope I was getting out of here without any wrist adornments.

Chapter 11

About five minutes after Zoe left, Jake came back into the room.

"Are you letting me go?" I asked.

He walked over, keys in hand. "Yes. Liam isn't going to press charges after all."

"Thanks. I appreciate you talking the cop who Tased me out of also putting me in jail," I said sarcastically.

Jake raised an eyebrow. "I managed to convince him you were going to be more trouble than it would be worth."

"This is why raising daughters to be polite and subservient never works."

"Well, a daughter raised to be polite and subservient probably never would have ended up in the position to grab a Taser off a cop in the first place," Jake pointed out.

"First of all, I didn't grab the Taser off him, I was trying to knock his hand away so he couldn't use it on a woman old enough to be my grandma. Secondly, you can't lecture me anymore. I'm a free woman."

"For now. I assume this means you're going to stop investigating James MacMahon's murder?"

"Sure. Assuming I was ever doing that in the first place. Which I wasn't."

Jake rolled his eyes. "Seriously? Please, stay out of my investigation. You're an amateur, you don't know what you're doing, and I really didn't want to spend my night babysitting you instead of looking for an actual killer. This is all that's happening now that there's a reward out; I'm spending my time getting my investigation blocked by people who don't know what they're doing and are just thinking of a payday."

"Well, maybe if your partner didn't Taser people just for being in a public park at night, you wouldn't have so many issues," I replied, crossing my arms. "Have you considered looking for actual criminals, like the murderer, instead? Sounds to me like Liam is the real amateur here."

Jake shook his head. "I've just uncuffed you, and you're still going to give me crap?"

"I should have never been arrested in the first place. But fine, go off and find your killer. I honestly do hope you find him. I don't like knowing I'm sharing an island with a murderer."

Jake nodded. "Yeah. We're doing our best."

"Now that I'm not under arrest, can Dorothy and Rosie come in?"

"It's past visiting hours, but following the rules

doesn't seem to be their strong suit, so as long as I don't get blamed for it, it's fine with me."

I grinned. "Thanks."

Jake nodded once more, pausing before he left the room. "I'm going to leave my card here. If by some chance you happen to come across anything that might help *me* solve this case, or if you remember anything that could help, can you let me know?"

I nodded, not telling Jake that I was immediately going to toss that card in the trash.

A few seconds later, Rosie and Dot rushed in. "Are you all right?" Rosie asked, concern written all over her face.

Dorothy, on the other hand, immediately gave me a high five. "I owe you a beer. I wouldn't have appreciated that much voltage, and I'm glad you took one for the team. I had my doubts about you, but I like you."

"Well, I'm glad thousands of volts of electricity coursing through my body was all it took," I replied, wincing as I tried to sit up in the bed.

"You're going to be all right for tomorrow, right?" Rosie asked. "After all, we still have to talk to Alice."

"I should be okay. I just need a few hours of sleep and half a bottle of Advil. And if I ask the nurses nicely, maybe they'll give me morphine."

"You can always hope," Dot laughed. "All right. Well, I'm glad you were with us tonight. And we still have that one clue, so you didn't get Tased for nothing."

"That would be the biggest shame of all," I said dryly.

"I'll talk to you in the morning. Do you want us to drop your car off somewhere?"

I smacked my forehead, remembering Mom had told me not to come home late because she wanted to get groceries.

"No, don't worry about it. I'll go grab it in the morning. Trust me, it'll be better for everyone."

"All right. We'll be in touch," Rosie said, and the two of them left, leaving me alone in the hospital room.

I figured that if the Taser hadn't killed me, my mom would when I got home.

AT EIGHT THE NEXT MORNING, I PULLED UP IN FRONT of Mom's place, feeling like I had been hit by a truck. I was going to have to walk to work or maybe order an Uber. I'd been checked out of the hospital and was trying to figure out what the odds were that I'd get fired if I called in sick after three days. Then I realized if Mom killed me first, it wasn't going to be an issue.

I walked through the front door, and Mom immediately rushed me. "There she is!" Taking me into a huge hug, Mom pulled me close to her.

"What? What's going on? Why are you hugging me? Do you have a knife?"

Mom pulled away and gave me a curious look. "What? Of course not. Why would I be mad?"

"I didn't bring your car back last night. Sorry. I got… distracted."

"Oh, what are groceries compared to knowing you

were getting it on with the man who might give me grandchildren one day?"

I groaned and pressed my hands against my face as I realized exactly why Mom wasn't mad: she thought I had hooked up with a guy.

And frankly, I wasn't past letting her think that was the truth.

"You look like he gave you a great workout last night, too."

I covered my ears as I went to the kitchen. "Yeah, and you know what I don't want to talk about at all? The last twelve hours of my life," I called back to her. "I'm just going to grab some coffee and go to work." Suddenly, spending the day scooping ice cream sounded far more pleasant than being here with my mom.

"You should have a quick shower first," Mom called out after me. "Unless you already showered with him, that is."

Completely ignoring her, I ran upstairs to the bathroom, shut the door, and wished there was a Taser nearby so I could just end it all this time.

Still, as awful as it was having Mom try and talk about all the sordid details of my non-affair, I under absolutely no conditions wanted her to know where I'd really spent last night.

I took a few minutes to enjoy the shower—the hot water on my sore body felt so good—then got out, threw on some clothes, and rushed back over to work, where Leslie raised her eyebrows as I came in.

"I was starting to wonder if you'd bailed on me."

"Sorry," I replied. "Long night."

"You look like hell."

"I've been through hell. But I've come back out the other side."

"Big night?"

"Yeah, but not in the way you think. Ten shots of Jägermeister would have been easier to deal with."

Leslie laughed. "Well, I always found a milkshake first thing was a good way to make a bad day better. Go ahead and make one before we get busy. I recommend making it with double chocolate brownie ice cream."

"I'm not going to say no to that," I replied with a grin. "Thanks."

Sure enough, a chocolate-heavy milkshake that sent sugar directly into my veins was exactly what I needed, and by the time we hit the first busy rush of the morning around ten, I was starting to feel half myself again.

During my break after the lunch rush, I checked my phone and saw I had a text from Rosie asking if I was still okay to have dinner that night.

Absolutely! I texted back.

I was more determined than ever to find the killer.

After a long day on my feet at the ice cream store, I headed home, had a quick shower, dressed in clothes that didn't have globs of raspberry crème brûlée ice cream on them, then drove over to Dot's apartment to meet up with her and Rosie.

"Oh, good, you dressed well," Dot said when I walked in through the front door.

"What did you think I was going to wear?"

Dot shrugged. "You never can know with your

generation. Something to look sexy in a TikTok video? Anyway, how are you feeling?"

"Like someone put a nice, warm blanket over me after I got hit by a truck. I'm getting better, but I'm not all the way there yet."

"Well, luckily, we're just having a fancy dinner, so there shouldn't be too many Tasers about," Rosie said. "I made a reservation, and we're going to be late."

TWENTY MINUTES LATER, THE THREE OF US WERE being led to a table by the edge of the balcony, over-looking the Pacific Ocean's turquoise waters. The soft sound of waves lapping against the shore mingled with the cool late-afternoon breeze, and I held my face to the wind, letting Maui's incredible natural power wash over me.

In some ways, no matter how much I resisted it, I still loved this island.

I fidgeted with the tablecloth for a moment, not used to something this fancy, before taking the menu handed to me by Rosie.

"Order whatever you'd like," Dot said. "After you stopped me from being Tased by a cop on a power trip last night, you've earned it. Besides, Rosie's paying."

I giggled as I scanned the restaurant, looking for Alice. I didn't see her, so my eyes moved to the menu, perusing the food options as I waited for the server.

I settled on a wood-fired pizza topped with prosciutto, rosemary cream sauce, and an egg and a large Coke Zero—I figured if we were going to talk to Alice, I wanted to be as sober as possible. Once the waiter left with our orders, I settled in to chat with Dot and Rosie.

"So how long have you lived on the island?" I asked them.

"My whole life," Dot replied. "Born and bred on Maui. Sure, I left a few times. The biggest mistake was following a man to Alaska. Never, ever leave a place you love for a man, Charlie. It's a bad idea. Especially Alaska." She gave an exaggerated shudder.

I laughed. "I've lived here since the sixties," Rosie replied. "Came from the mainland before that. I grew up in New York."

"Ah," I said with a nod. "Cool. You like it here?"

"Oh, yes. It's very different from where I used to live, but I love everything about life here. It's all very simple."

I nodded. Life on the island could be simple. Of course, it was even more so when I didn't have to live with my mother.

The waiter arrived with our food then, but I didn't even pay attention to the amazing-smelling pizza he was putting in front of me; my eyes were on the woman behind him being led to a nearby table by the waitress. That was Alice. No question.

As soon as the waiter left, I pointed her out to the others.

"Well, we may as well enjoy this meal for now," Rosie said. "Let's follow her when she leaves and speak with her then."

After enjoying the most incredible pizza of my life—

seriously, I'd never been to Italy, but I imagine that must be what pizza there tasted like—I got to spend some more time with Dot and Rosie as we waited for Alice to finish her own meal. To be honest, I hadn't really imagined they'd be all that much fun to hang out with. After all, they were older than my grandparents, but it turned out they were also cool as anything. Dot knew everything to do with computers, and Rosie was quieter and more serious but had a real caring streak about her. She gave me the impression that I could come to her with anything. She was whip smart, too. She tried to hide it, but behind that somewhat passive exterior was a woman with a sharp wit and a very good memory.

About half an hour after we finished eating, Alice got up from her seat, and the three of us followed. Instead of going back into the hotel, however, she took the lit path toward the beach, and this was our chance.

"Excuse me, dear," Rosie said.

Alice spun to face us. "Yes?"

She was obviously stressed. Her makeup hid it well, but I could see the dark circles under her eyes, and her hair was a little bit more haggard than it had looked in most of her Instagram pictures. She pressed her lips together as she looked at us, the tension in her shoulders obvious.

"You're the assistant to that poor man who was killed the other day, aren't you?"

Alice narrowed her eyes at us. "Who wants to know?"

"This woman here, her name's Charlotte, she was the last person besides the taxi driver to see your boss alive, and we were wondering if we might ask you about him. Only if you'd like, of course."

Alice looked at me carefully. "You were, were you?"

I nodded. "Yeah. He came into the ice cream shop I work at so I could call him an Uber. His account had been hacked."

"Okay, you're not lying," she said. "Come with me."

The three of us walked along the beach for a few minutes in silence. Alice eventually sat down in the sand, and the three of us followed her lead. I buried my feet deep, past the sun-heated top layer and down to where it was cool and fresh.

"It had been such a hectic afternoon," Alice said in a soft voice. "Normally, in that situation, I would have just ordered the Uber for him, but I was trying to get James on a flight back to New York. We had originally planned on spending the night here, but another one of his projects, a new hotel in Philly, had an emergency meeting related to zoning, and James wanted to be there himself. The problem was, on such short notice, it was hard to get a flight off the islands. Everything was booked. So I was busy calling the airlines and told James to sort his own ride to the airport. I figured that was better. God, if only I'd ordered the Uber."

I shook my head. "I don't think it would have made a difference."

"You don't think the cab driver killed him?" Alice asked, looking at me sharply.

I shook my head. "No, I don't think so. I saw the cabbie. He was shaken up, and he didn't even know who your boss was. Neither did I until I saw it in the papers."

Alice shook her head. "It was so ridiculous, this whole hotel. It wasn't my place to say, but it was such a bad idea."

"You really think so?" Dorothy asked.

Alice nodded. "He was getting threats. He always laughed them off like they were nothing, but I wasn't so sure. People here really hated that project. James always told me it would grow on them, that people always hate change, but they get used to it in the end. 'People hated the Empire State Building when it first went up,' he would tell me." Alice shook her head. "I never imagined…" She trailed off and looked at the water.

"Did you keep copies of the threats?"

Alice nodded. "Yeah. Most of them came by email or through Facebook or like that. It was really rare to have one physically mailed to his office."

"I'd appreciate if you could forward them all on to me," Dorothy said.

"I can, sure. Are you trying to find who killed him?"

"We are," Rosie said.

"Well, you seem a lot nicer than all the people messaging me. I've had to change all my social media accounts to private and block people from messaging me," Alice said. "I keep getting random messages from people wanting to meet up."

"Sorry to hear that," Dorothy said. "Now, we heard James had an argument with Calvin at lunch that day."

"He sure did," Alice said. "I thought Calvin was going to have a stroke right there at the table. I get why he was mad, but that was business."

"Do you think he could have been mad enough to kill James?" I asked Alice.

She bit her lip as she thought about it for a moment. "You know, I wouldn't have thought so. But then, I suppose you never really know what someone is capable of, do you? James going back on their agreement was going to cost Calvin's company tens of millions of dollars. I guess that's probably enough for someone to kill over."

"Who else did James know on the island?" I asked. "After all, being from New York, there can't be that many people."

"All the county councilmembers," Alice said immediately. "He met with them quite a few times, along with the mayor of Maui County, of course. He knows a handful of the town organizers, although mostly just to say hello to. And then there's Calvin and a few other businesspeople around town."

"Anyone he's ever had an issue with?" Dorothy asked.

Alice shook her head. "No. For a cutthroat businessman, James made a point of getting along with everyone he could. There was bad news given from time to time, of course, like with Calvin the other day, but for the most part, James was a likeable guy. He had charisma. I really liked him."

That fit with what I'd seen from the man at the ice cream shop. He certainly had that aura of a man who did his best to get along with everyone.

"Was there anything to this rumor that James bribed

people on the council to get the project allowed through?" I asked.

Alice pursed her lips. "Look, I can't say for sure. I don't *know* for sure. But I can say that the opposition from locals on this project was so strong that I have to believe any councilperson who voted in favor of the project either doesn't want to have a job next time the elections come around, or someone made it worth their while to tank their political careers. Beyond that, I don't have a clue."

Alice sighed and looked out over the water before she continued. "You know what I want more than anything? To go home. I'm scared of being on this island. Someone wanted James dead, and they killed him, and I don't know why, but it had to be business related. I'm his assistant. What if James knew something he shouldn't have found out, and they're afraid he told me? What if I'm next? The truth is I haven't left the hotel grounds because of it. I'm scared, and I want to go home."

"When are you scheduled to go back?" Rosie asked softly, putting her hand on Alice's.

The younger woman didn't pull away. "In a few days," Alice replied. "Honestly, it's been nice to talk to you. I don't have anyone in my life to talk to right now. I don't want to admit to my friends and family what's going on."

"Strangers can be good that way," Dot said. "By all means, tell us whatever you're thinking. We'll listen to you no matter what."

"I just hope someone finds who killed him. That

would make me feel a lot better. Will you do that for me?"

"We'll do our best," I said softly. "We really will."

Alice nodded and stood up once more. "Thank you. For being here, for talking to me. I appreciate it."

"Can you think of anyone else on the island—or in the state—who might have wanted James dead?" Rosie asked again. "Any business associates at all who might have had enough of the project?"

"I'm afraid I can't," Alice said. "I genuinely don't think he had problems with anyone apart from Calvin."

"All right. Thanks."

Alice nodded and went back into the hotel, while the three of us stayed on the beach for another few minutes, thinking through what we'd just learned.

Chapter 12

"**W**hat do you think?" Rosie asked after a few minutes.

"I think the first thing we need to find out is whether Calvin was on Maui that night," I said. "If he flew back to Oahu—and stayed there—that night, then we can rule him out as a suspect. But if he stayed on the island, he's my main guy."

"I have a friend who works for Hawaiian Airlines," Dot said. "I can ask her to check the passenger logs. She'll tell me when he went back to Oahu."

"I think we need to look into the councilmembers," Rosie said.

"Janice Evers is retiring, and she voted in favor of the project," I chimed in. "So did Natalie Lee. If anyone took a bribe, I bet it was her. I know that much."

Dot nodded. "Yes. But there are five councilmembers in Maui County. Albert Millner also voted for the project."

"Is he retiring?" I asked.

"Not as far as I know. The next election isn't for eighteen months, though."

"I wonder if James bribed all of them," I mused.

"It's possible," Dot said. "Maybe he reneged on the deal afterward. I think it's also something we need to look into. Those are our two best approaches."

"Agreed," Rosie said. "Are you working tomorrow?"

I nodded. "Yeah, but I'm usually done around three."

"Good. We'll reconvene afterward."

The three of us got up and left, with Rosie and Dot dropping me off at Mom's car before I headed home. I was just walking through the door when I got a text from Zoe.

Well, it was nice to show up to work and see that you haven't been Tased and arrested again.

As I sent her back a whole bunch of the tongue-sticking-out emojis, Mom called out to me. "Are you going out again tonight? Maybe you're going to see that man again?"

"Nope," I replied. "I'm having a night in."

"Well, I suppose that's good. You don't want him to think you're too easy. Giving it up two nights in a row just makes you seem desperate."

"Weren't you going to go grocery shopping?" I asked, my voice involuntarily rising an octave. "I need some Oreos, if you don't mind buying a pack."

I didn't need Oreos. What I *did* need was for my mom to start talking about literally *anything* other than my nonexistent sex life.

"I can do that. Normal Oreos?"

"Can you get the birthday cake ones if they have them?" I asked with a grin. Birthday cake Oreos were my secret guilty pleasure.

"Sure. Anything else? I was thinking of making quesadillas for dinner."

Grateful that the conversation had moved on, I shook my head. "Nothing specific, thanks. Maybe just a few snacks to graze on. I already ate, so I'm not super hungry."

"Will do. I'll be back in an hour."

"Thanks, Mom."

Once Mom left, I decided to take Coco out for a walk down to the beach. As soon as we left the house, she began straining against her harness in the right direction, and I laughed. It hadn't taken long for my little dog to figure out exactly where the beach was. She wasn't the biggest fan of the water—once she went in and a six-inch wave surprised her—but she loved running along the sand, sniffing every inch of the beach, digging holes, and meeting all sorts of new dog friends.

The sun was just beginning to set, as we'd had dinner so early it still wasn't dark out, and I enjoyed yet another gorgeous Maui sunset on the beach as I looked out at the waves. The ocean seemed to beckon me, but a part of me wanted to resist its siren call.

Dad had always loved the ocean. He had wanted to teach me how to surf when I was little, but I'd hated it. I was the kid who wanted to stay indoors and play with my toys. Zoe had been the one who was always outside, always on the beach. At school, she would show me the different shells she'd found.

Meanwhile, Dad would go out in the morning and surf, and if he made me come, I would stay in the car, where the sand couldn't get into all of my clothes.

Tears stung my eyes as I wished I'd gone surfing with him. Even just once.

As if sensing my emotional state Coco ran over to me, tail wagging, and rubbed herself up against my leg. I laughed, wiping away my tears as I reached down to pat my happy little dog. Coco was the best dog in the whole world, and I was so grateful to have her in my life.

"Dad would have loved you," I whispered to her as I picked up a stick and threw it down the beach. Coco wagged her tail as hard as she could as she rushed after it.

We were heading home when I got a text from Zoe.

Hey, are you up for a chat?

Sure, I replied.

I'm going to come over. Let's get ice cream or something. I need to talk to you about a problem I'm having.

I walked home with Coco and Zoe showed up about ten minutes later. I hopped into the passenger seat of her car while she drove us to Dairy Queen. Zoe got a Blizzard while I went for my favorite—a Peanut Buster Parfait—and parked nearby before we got out of the car and headed toward the beach.

"So what's going on?" I asked.

Zoe sighed. "I've got a creep after me."

"A guy?"

She nodded. "Yeah."

"Great. Tell me all about it."

"He was a patient at the hospital about two weeks

ago. He came in with pain in his back, he was diagnosed with kidney stones, and I gave him some pain medication and sent him on his way. The CT scan showed they were tiny and he'd have no problem passing them on his own. I figured that was the last I'd see of him, but then last week, he was waiting for me outside the hospital after my shift. He asked me out and tried to get my number, but I refused and told him I had a boyfriend. He called me a bitch and left. Not the worst thing a guy's ever called me, but whatever. I wrote it off, thinking that was the end of it."

I nodded. It wouldn't be the first time a man who thought he was entitled to a woman's phone number called her a bitch, and it certainly wouldn't be the last. "But it wasn't?"

Zoe shook her head. "Last week, one of the other nurses told me he tried to get my number from her. So I called hospital security, and he's been banned from the premises. I called the cops as well to file a report, but they told me they couldn't do anything because there was no pattern of harassment."

"Oh, yeah, let's just wait until he attacks you before doing anything," I said, rolling my eyes.

"Right? Not that I like to think about that too much. But they were not interested at all. I stopped thinking about him for a bit, what with the excitement of you coming back to the island and then you ending up in the hospital, and the murder. Then, when I got home from my shift last night, I saw him in my building's parking lot."

I gasped. "No!"

Zoe nodded. "It was him. I'm one hundred percent sure of it. I don't know how he found me. I don't know if he followed me after work one day without me noticing, but he was at my building. Where I *live*. And I'm not going to lie, Charlie. I'm scared."

I looked over at my friend, and worry was written all over her face. Her eyes looked at me desperately, searching for a solution.

"Okay," I said. "First things first. We're going back to my place, and we're switching cars. If he's still there, he might know what you drive, but he won't know what I drive. Mom should be back with the groceries by now. We're going to sneak up on him, and then we're going to scare him into leaving you alone."

"Are you serious?" Zoe asked. "This had better not involve anything illegal."

"Don't worry," I replied. "It's not illegal if you know what you're doing is wrong."

"That is… absolutely not how the law works."

"You're such a stickler for the rules. Don't worry. I won't commit any *real* crimes. Just, you know, maybe a light misdemeanor."

"This is a bad idea," Zoe groaned.

"No, it's an excellent idea. You've got a stalker, and the cops aren't going to help, so we have to get rid of him ourselves."

"Seriously, I don't want us breaking the law."

"Fine. We'll just break his legs."

Zoe shot me a look.

"*Fine.* We won't break anything on him. But we have to make sure he knows to stay away from you."

Sure enough, once we got back to my place, Mom had come back with the groceries, so I grabbed the car, and Zoe and I drove to her place.

"I don't know what to do," she said. "I really don't. What if he won't leave me alone?"

"Then we'll deal with that when we get there," I said firmly. "Do you know his name?"

"Yeah," Zoe said. "And his address. I know it from the hospital. What if he won't leave me alone, though?"

"We'll cross that bridge when we get to it," I replied. "Where to from here?"

"Just take a left down here."

I hadn't realized Zoe only lived a few blocks away from Dot. Her building looked a little bit newer, and if I'd had to guess, I'd have said it was built in the nineties. The exterior and yard were both well maintained; this was definitely a building where professionals lived. I pulled into a visitor's parking slot as Zoe looked around.

"His car is gone."

"Are you sure?" I asked.

She nodded. "Yeah. He was in a red Ford Escort." Zoe leaned back against the seat and sighed. "I don't like this, Charlie. I don't like this at all."

"Okay," I said. "I know. It sucks. Let's go inside, and you're going to pack a bag. You're staying with me tonight."

"I don't like feeling like a prisoner when this is my home," Zoe said.

I nodded. "I agree. You shouldn't have to, and hopefully it won't be for long. We'll take care of it. But for now, your safety is the most important thing. Come on."

The two of us got out of the car, and I could tell Zoe was on tenterhooks as we walked toward the building, her head scanning from side to side constantly, as if she expected the man stalking her to dart out from the shadows. It wasn't fair at all that someone was making my best friend feel this unsafe, and I felt the urge to punch this guy.

Zoe and I climbed the stairs to the second floor of the building. "I'd have expected a place this new to have elevators," I said as we reached the top.

"Oh, it does," Zoe replied breezily.

"What? Then why did we take the stairs?"

"Because there's, like, ten of them, and it's good for you. Are you seriously puffed because you went up one flight of stairs?"

"No," I lied, doing my best to sound casually offended despite the fact it was completely true.

"Okay, seriously, we're going to the gym together at some point."

We reached the door to Zoe's apartment, and she opened it. I couldn't help but hold my breath, but it was completely empty. I had been half expecting the crazy stalker to be inside.

"Pack up some things," I told her. "I'm going to call a cop that I know."

Zoe raised an eyebrow. "You know a cop here in Maui? Is it the one who Tased you?"

"No," I replied. "It's his partner. And I know it's not a great situation. But someone needs to take this seriously, and you're not getting anywhere by just calling up the station, so I'm pulling some strings where I can."

I rummaged through my purse until I found the card Jake had given me. I had planned on throwing it out immediately, but then I'd figured I never knew when it would come in handy. And now was that time. The card had his phone number on it, and I dialed.

"Hello. Jacob Llewelyn speaking," he answered.

"Hi, Jake. It's Charlie. The woman your partner Tased for no reason the other day."

There was a pause on the other end of the line. I was pretty sure he was taking some deep breaths. "Hi. How's it going? Do you have anything for me?"

"Actually, I have a favor to ask."

"Does this favor involve you doing or having done anything illegal? I'm not bailing you out of another arrest."

"Relax. I'm only going to be doing something illegal if you cops won't protect my friend."

"What's going on?"

I explained the entire situation to him, including the fact that the police officers wouldn't take Zoe's report.

"What's the address? I'll be there soon."

"Meet me at my place instead," I said, rattling off Mom's home address. "Neither one of us wants to be here for longer than we have to be."

"Understood," Jake said. "Call me if you see anything suspicious. And I'm telling you, Charlie, what-ever happens, do *not* approach this guy."

"That's not going to stop him from approaching us."

"Let's hope it doesn't come to that. I'll see you soon."

I hung up the phone as Zoe came out with a duffel

bag packed with clothes. The stress was written all over her face. "Okay, I've got it."

"Good. When we get back to Mom's place, there's a cop who's going to be there, ready to take your statement. It sounds like he's actually taking this seriously."

Zoe shot me a grateful look. "You're amazing, Charlie. You're always taking care of me."

"Seriously, what are friends for? I would help you bury a body. And it sounds like that might become a very real possibility."

"I hope not."

"I listen to so many murder podcasts, I am not letting my best friend become a victim," I said firmly. "Listening to your gut and pushing to make sure you're getting help is how you get out of this without ending up as a feature when *My Favorite Murder* does a live show in Honolulu."

"This conversation isn't making me feel better," Zoe said.

"Okay, but Jake will," I replied, leading her out of the apartment.

She locked the door, and we headed back down to the car, both of us scanning the parking lot as we left to make sure the stalker hadn't returned.

"What's his name, anyway?" I asked when we were back on the road.

"Josh. Josh Newman. He listed one of the hotels in Wailea as his employer. That's all I know about him, apart from the fact that he's gotten kidney stones once in his life."

I nodded. "Sounds like a bad dude. I hope the stones hurt to pass."

"I think the oath I took means I'm not allowed to hope for that," Zoe said, allowing herself a small smile.

I reached over and placed my hand on hers. "Don't worry. You're safe now."

"Are you sure it's going to be okay for me to come to your place? I can always go to my parents' place."

"They live, like, an hour away, right? That's too far. Mom lives ten minutes from here. Besides, she loves you. I'm pretty sure she'd be thrilled if you were her daughter instead of me."

"Oh, that's not true," Zoe said with a laugh. "It is easier though. I know Mom and Dad love it out Hana way since they retired, but it's not nearly as convenient for me."

"Come on," I said, turning off the car after I parked in front of Mom's house. A sleek, newish sedan in front of the house told me Jake was already here. "It's going to be fine. And Jake is here. He'll make sure this Josh guy gets driven away."

"I hope you're right," Zoe said with a sigh as she climbed out of the car.

Chapter 13

When we walked into the house, Jake was in the living room, sitting on the couch with a beer, while my mom sat in the armchair across from him. As soon as she saw us, her face lit up.

"Why, Charlotte dear, how *lovely* of you to bring home your new man to meet me."

My mouth dropped open as I realized what was happening and just how powerless I was to stop it. I really hoped Jake hadn't been here long.

"Mom, it's not what you think…"

"Now, I've just been speaking to Jake about you. I've let him know that you have great birthing hips, just like me. Plus, it's always more fun in the bedroom that way, but I'm sure he knows all about that already," she said, flashing him a wink.

The expression on Jake's face seemed halfway between abject horror and morbid amusement.

"Mom, get out," I said, pointing my finger toward

the door. "He's not my boyfriend, he's a cop, and he's here to take a statement."

"Well, the two don't have to be mutually exclusive," Mom replied. "After all, he is pretty good-looking, and you can always play with his handcuffs."

"He's going to have to investigate a murder if you don't get out of this room and stop talking right now," I replied. "Yours."

"All right, all right. Though that's no way to speak to your mother."

"What you just said to him was no way to speak to your daughter's *husband*, let alone a guy she barely knows," I shot back, completely mortified.

"Well, I'll let the two of you get to know each other a bit better, then," Mom said, winking at Jake.

I resisted the urge to grab a vase off the nearby side table and throw it at her as she left.

"By the way, Zoe is staying with us tonight," I shouted after her as Mom went back into the kitchen.

"All right, I'll set up the guest room."

Zoe and I sat down on the couch across from Jake, who looked like he was enjoying himself far too much. A grin spread across his face, and his chest moved up and down as if he was trying to hide the fact that he was laughing.

"You stop that," I snapped at him.

"Sorry," he said with a laugh. "I'm no stranger to women trying to hit on me in this job—I swear, the badge is an aphrodisiac to some people—but your mom is on a whole new level."

"You don't need to tell me," I muttered. "I should

have warned you before you came, but my mind was on other things. Like the stalker following Zoe."

"Right." Jake was instantly back into cop mode, and he pulled out his notebook and flipped it open, leaning forward. "First of all, I need your personal information."

Zoe gave him her name, phone number, and address then recounted the entire story to Jake.

To his credit, he seemed to be taking it very seriously. "He hasn't approached you personally since you told him to leave you alone outside the hospital, though?" Jake eventually asked.

Zoe shook her head. "No. But I mean, he was in the parking lot of my building. He obviously found out where I lived. That's stalking, isn't it?"

"A case can be made for it," Jake replied. "I would certainly apply for an order of protection. When you submit your application, a temporary restraining order will be instituted, and he won't even have to be in court for it. About two weeks later, you'll get a hearing on the TRO, at which point he can attempt to show cause that the restraining order isn't necessary."

"How do I get one?" Zoe asked quietly.

"Go to the family court anytime," Jake replied. "If you want, I can find you an attorney who will help you with the filing. They'll do it for free."

"Thanks, but it's okay," Zoe said with a small smile. "I know a lawyer who can help."

"Good."

"But a temporary restraining order won't do anything if he decides to actually attack her, right?" I asked. "I mean, you're just telling him to stay away. If he's really dangerous, what then?"

"I can't arrest someone because they might commit a crime in the future," Jake said. "I know sometimes it's not ideal, especially when you feel as if you're in danger, like Zoe here, but unfortunately my hands are tied on the matter. I think having her stay here for a few days at least is a good plan."

"Great. So you're basically saying there's a psycho out there, and the only thing we can do is hope he doesn't do anything bad to her."

"When the TRO is issued, if he shows up at the hospital or her home again, you can call the police and have him picked up," Jake said. "For most men like this, the TRO is enough. They're creeps who don't understand that no means no, but usually a piece of paper from the cops is enough to get them to move on."

"It's fine, Charlie," Zoe said, putting a hand on my arm. "I'm sure Jake is right. I'll get the TRO, he'll get the hint, and he'll leave me alone."

"Okay," I replied. "But you're switching cars with my mom and staying here until this is all sorted out."

"All right," Zoe said.

"I'll head over to the station and write up an official report," Jake said. "You'll be able to take it to family court to help your request. I don't suppose you got the names of the officers who refused to treat this seriously, did you?"

Zoe shook her head. "Sorry."

"It's not important. But if there's someone at the station who refuses to take harassing behavior against women on this island seriously, I want to know about it. What Newman did counts as harassment, and a report should have been filed. I'm sorry for your experience."

I had to admit, I was surprised by Jake's reaction to the police not caring. Given that his partner had attempted to Taser a seventy-plus-year-old woman less than twenty-four hours ago, I had kind of figured that he would be one of those cops who'd gone into that career for the chance to legally beat people up with a nightstick. Even when he'd convinced his partner to not press charges against me, I had assumed it was because he'd gotten the sense I would have put up a fight and made it as ugly as I could.

I figured he would come and take Zoe's statement because he did seem to actually do his job, but I hadn't expected him to go beyond that and look into the cops who hadn't. I was pleased to see my initial assessment might not have been exactly spot on.

He stood up then.

I did the same. "I'll walk you out so you don't accidentally end up alone with my mother again," I said.

"And I'll check to see how she's doing with the room and keep her out of your way," Zoe said to me quietly, and I shot her a grateful look.

"Your mother sure is something," Jake said to me as we walked to the door.

I rolled my eyes. "Yeah, that's the understatement of the year. I wish I had one of those mothers that just passive-aggressively hinted to her children that they want grandbabies. My mother skipped the passive part and is just straight-up aggressive about it."

"You're not wrong. She asked me what my preferred name for a son would be."

I let out a groan. "Ugh. Sorry. What did you tell her?"

"That I liked the name Oliver," Jake said with a grin. "Listen, I'll have a copy of the report emailed to Zoe in half an hour."

I nodded. "Mom has a printer here she can use."

"It's good she can stay here. The TRO will probably be enough to scare this guy off, but until then, I don't want Zoe to be in any more danger than she has to be."

I nodded. "Agreed. Thanks for coming out. I figure taking regular reports isn't exactly in your purview as a detective."

"It's still a police matter. And the fact is Zoe should have been listened to the other times she called the police. It's ridiculous that she wasn't."

I agreed. "On *My Favorite Murder*, it comes up far too often that people called the cops, nothing happened, and then the person was killed."

"You're a fan of true crime, huh? I guess that explains a lot."

"And what exactly does that mean?"

"That you feel it's appropriate and safe for you to investigate a murder and find someone who has killed somebody just because you listen to two women tell stories of other people being murdered and their killers being found."

"Hey, the killers aren't always found," I retorted, but the point stung. He was right, and I knew it. And okay, they were always saying that people should stay out of murder investigations, too. But this was different.

"That wasn't the point."

"Do you have a better way to make a hundred grand?"

"Literally anything that doesn't involve both impeding a murder investigation and having a high chance of your body ending up washed up on the beach?"

"Unfortunately, literally anything else only pays minimum wage."

"The risk of death at the hands of a murderer is a lot lower though."

"Respect the hustle," I replied.

Jake rolled his eyes. "I mean it, Charlie. I don't want to see you get hurt. Please, stop looking into this murder. Take care of your friend. She needs you right now."

I frowned. "Okay," I replied. Inside, I was thinking, *but I can do two things at once.*

Satisfied, Jake nodded. "I'll be in touch."

I closed the door behind him, trying to ignore the flock of butterflies that seemed to have spontaneously developed in my stomach.

"It's probably just the idea of handcuffs," I muttered to myself as I went back toward the guest room.

Mom had gotten out some towels for Zoe. "You stay here as long as you need," she was saying. "It's so nice to see you around again, Zoe. You'll have to tell me all about your job sometime. It's so impressive that you're a doctor now. I always knew you'd be something great.

You always had your head in a book, even while Charlie was trying to get you into trouble."

"Thanks, Carmen," Zoe said. "I really appreciate it. It's nice to see you as well. And I promise, Charlie didn't get me into trouble."

"Oh, I heard the stories," Mom said, wagging her finger. "Now, don't you girls stay up too late; you both have to work in the morning. Oh, how I've missed saying those words, although of course it was all about school then."

I laughed. "Thanks, Mom."

"There's food in the kitchen if you need it. I made quesadillas, so help yourselves."

"We will."

Mom left, and I plonked myself down on the armchair across from the bed while Zoe unpacked. "So, how are you feeling?" I asked her. "Are you holding up okay?"

"Yeah. Thanks for getting that cop to come here. He's the one who was at the hospital, right?"

"His partner Tased me. He didn't seem quite as bad."

"No," Zoe said with a laugh. "Better looking, too."

"Oh, don't you start," I said with a wag of my finger. "I get enough of that from Mom."

"Hey, I'm the one who's used Tinder on this island. Pickings are slim, I'm telling you, and I gave up a long time ago. If you find a guy that good looking, with a steady job, who also believes that stalking women is a bad thing, hold onto him is all I'm saying."

I laughed. "Well, you can have him, then."

"Sorry, too busy working and trying to keep weird psychos away from me."

"Fair enough."

"But seriously, tonight made me feel way better about things. I'm going to call my mom, and first thing tomorrow, we'll go to family court and get the TRO."

"Good," I said to her. "I'll let you call her."

I left the room and went down to the kitchen to grab a bit of food before heading to bed. I had a feeling tomorrow was going to be another big day.

Chapter 14

The following morning, I woke up a little late and decided that breakfast could wait. After all, Leslie always let me have free ice cream during my shift, and if I made a milkshake with the scrumptious blueberry cheesecake flavor, the fruit basically made it count as a smoothie. And smoothies are healthy.

I said goodbye to Mom, while Zoe decided to give me a ride in to work, since she had to meet her mom at the courthouse anyway.

"Are you sure you're going to be okay?" I asked her.

She nodded. "Yeah, thanks. I appreciate the help. You're a good friend. Stay out of trouble, okay?"

"I always do my best," I replied with a wink.

"Do you, though?" Zoe asked with a teasing chuckle.

I stuck my tongue out at her. "Well, now I'm not going to offer you a free scoop of ice cream if you come in."

Zoe's shoulders slumped. "Well, I guess I deserved

that. Anyway, I hope you have a nice day. I'm working until eight, so I won't see you until later tonight."

"Cool. I might be out late as well. I'm meeting up with some new friends that I'm working with to solve the murder."

Zoe's eyebrows rose. "The two women who were waiting for you at the hospital?"

I nodded.

"I hadn't picked them as the type who would be involved in a murder investigation. Still, they seemed nice."

"They're… weird. But I like them."

"As long as they mostly keep you out of trouble, I like them too," Zoe said with a grin.

"Sure. As long as 'mostly' is the key word in that sentence. I'll talk to you later. Text me if you need anything. Anything at all."

Zoe smiled at me. "You're the best."

I HEADED IN TO WORK, WHERE LESLIE WAS MORE THAN happy to have me make my morning "smoothie," which tasted like a delicious, creamy version of a cheesecake. I sipped it in between helping customers, who consisted mostly of tourists, but there were a few regulars who lived in the neighborhood that I was beginning to recognize.

"Hey," I said to one woman, Jess, about my age, who came in every few days after her run. Her headphones hung around her neck, and a thin sheen of sweat always covered her skin. She was slim, always wearing a pair of lululemon shorts and a shirt, her long blonde hair tied in a ponytail. A part of me kind of wanted to hate her for being so perfect, but she was so nice I just couldn't bring myself to do it.

"Hi, Charlie," she greeted me, then held up a hand and took a big swig from the water bottle she held at her side. "Sorry. The humidity's really getting to me today."

"So you *are* human," I said with a good-natured laugh.

Jess chuckled. "Unfortunately, yes. But if I'm going to qualify for Boston next year, I need to shave ten minutes off my PR, and that means running even when it's humid."

"What time do you have to hit to make Boston?" I asked. Twenty-six miles in anything under about six hours sounded good to me.

"Three and a half hours on the dot," Jess replied.

I let the scoop of ice cream I was holding drop right back into the bucket. "You are kidding. Like, that's for the whole marathon? Not just the first ten miles?"

Jess laughed. "It is. I managed three hours forty-one last year at Honolulu. I'm this close to it."

"No kidding. You can do it, for sure."

"I hope you're right. I've got my plan for next year. Deadline is in September, so I missed it this time, but I'll get there."

"You will," I said, nodding.

"I'd have a better chance if I didn't eat ice cream

after every run, but I mean, I just ran ten miles. I kind of feel like I deserve it."

"Honey, I tell myself I deserve ice cream for managing to show up to work on time," I replied. "You deserve an entire tub of this stuff for that effort."

Jess laughed. "Well, if I did that, I'd never make Boston, unfortunately."

I handed her the cup of her regular order—a single scoop of toffee and chocolate chip in a burnt-sugar base with caramel swirl—and Jess handed over some cash.

"Thanks for this," she said. "This is the best part of my day. Do you run?"

"Only if I'm chasing the nearest ice cream truck."

"You should try it. You don't have to be fast. But it's good exercise."

I smiled. "Exercise isn't really my thing."

"Only because you haven't found a way to enjoy it," Jess said airily.

"Yeah, that's probably true."

"We live in Hawaii. This is the perfect place to live an active life. If you ever want to come for a run with me one day, let me know."

"Thanks," I said, smiling. "I will."

I was never, ever going to take her up on that offer, as nice as Jess was. Running was not for me.

Jess flashed me a smile and waved as she left. I wondered if she had grown up on the island. I hadn't known her as a kid, but I liked her.

The more time I spent on this island, the more I realized I liked a lot of the people here. I had been so happy here while I was growing up. When Dad died, we'd moved away where Mom could get work, and I was really glad for it. It had hurt too much to stay here then. When I'd come back, it had fully been with the intention of this being a temporary thing. I was just going to lie low until things cooled off in Seattle. It couldn't take *that* long before the gangsters forgot about me, surely. A year, tops.

But the more time I spent here, the more I was reminded of just why I had loved this place so much. The weather was incredible. The sunsets were second to none. But more importantly, the people were the friendliest I'd ever met. Strangers would talk to you in the street about anything. Neighbors looked out for one another. No one rushed past, stressed to hit a deadline or a timetable, like they did on the Mainland. Island time was a very real thing, and I enjoyed it so much more than Seattle.

Maybe, just maybe I could consider staying here a little bit longer than I'd originally planned.

Before I could think about it further, my next customer of the day came up, obviously a tourist, and as soon as she demanded samples of three different flavors to start with, I knew it was going to take a while to serve her.

By the end of the day I was exhausted, and hungry—I had skipped lunch, and the milkshake I'd had for breakfast made up the only food I'd eaten so far today—so I grabbed a burger from a drive-through before texting Rosie.

We tracked down Calvin Monroe. He's going to see a movie later tonight with his wife. You in?

Of course, I texted back a moment later. *I just finished up work now.*

Meet us at Dorothy's.

Be there in five.

I sent Zoe a quick text, just checking in to see how the courthouse had gone, and then drove over to Dorothy's place. I was halfway there when a bing from my phone told me Zoe had replied, and once I finally parked the car, I pulled it out from my purse to see what she said.

It went well! I was really pleased. I'm feeling much less stressed.

I smiled as I read her message and replied, *I'm glad to hear it.*

I headed up into the building and knocked on the door, and Dot let me in.

"Good, you're here."

"How did you find out about Calvin Monroe's date night?"

"We have our methods," Rosie replied, tapping her nose and winking at me. "They mostly involve being so old that I know half the people who live on this island, including the mother of the woman working as a nanny for the Monroe family back on Oahu. But you didn't hear that from me."

"Hear what from you?" I replied, and Rosie gave me an approving nod.

"Good. Do you have the day off tomorrow?"

"No, but I can ask Leslie if I can leave early if necessary. What's up?"

"There's a meeting of county councilmembers at three thirty."

"I'll be there," I said.

We spent some time discussing the case, trying to get closer to an answer, and when five thirty rolled around, the three of us headed down to the Regal Maui Megaplex.

"What movie are they seeing?" I asked.

"Some romcom with Ryan Reynolds and Emma Stone," Rosie said, blowing a raspberry and making a thumbs-down motion.

I laughed. "Not a fan of romantic comedy?" I asked.

Rosie shook her head. "No chance. Give me a good old spy thriller any day of the week. Jason Bourne movies might be inaccurate as anything, but they're a lot of fun. Why couldn't they have wanted to see the new Jack Reacher movie?"

"Agreed. That's much more romantic," Dot said. "No one cares about some guy who's trying to turn into a better barista for his girlfriend, but everyone loves a man who's willing to save the planet."

I laughed at Dot's idea of a romantic movie. "I can see why neither one of you are married."

"Hey, I *was* married, but my husband didn't love me enough to have a ticker that lasted him past fifty," Dot said.

"Oh, I'm sorry," I blurted, feeling bad for having put my foot in my mouth once again.

She waved aside my apology. "Don't be. He died so long ago, and frankly, he was a controlling ass. I'm not speaking ill of the dead, but my life's been a lot more pleasant since he hasn't been in it."

We reached the front of the ticket line then, and Rosie paid for everyone's tickets. I mouthed her my thanks, and she shot me a wink in reply as Dot grabbed my arm and pulled me toward the concession counter.

"This is my favorite part of the movies. I want to get popcorn. I never make popcorn at home."

"You know, you're an adult. There's no one stopping you."

"I know, but the popcorn you get at the movies really feels like it's going directly into your arteries. You just can't get that same flavor that tastes so fake and yet so delicious at the same time in your kitchen," Dot said. I couldn't argue with that.

We arrived at the seats, loaded up with popcorn, candy, and copious amounts of pop, and Rosie raised her eyebrows when she saw us. "Haven't eaten anything in the past week, have we?"

"Hey, I don't get to go to the movies enough anymore. The calories don't count when you can't see yourself eating them, anyway," Dot replied.

I smiled as I started munching on a bit of popcorn, and Rosie leaned in close and pointed out a couple sitting three rows in front of us.

"That's Calvin and his wife," she said. "We won't be able to speak to them during the movie, of course. But he bought an extra-large Coke, which he's currently sipping on, so I think odds are good he's going to have to take a trip to the little boys' room during the movie."

The lights dimmed then, signaling the start of the movie, and I settled in.

Chapter 15

Unlike my two companions, I was all about terrible romantic comedies—and good ones as well. And since my financial situation, combined with my romantic entanglement situation—or lack thereof—didn't result in me getting a lot of opportunities to see them in theatres, I was going to enjoy myself. After all, sitting in a theatre with a giant bag of deliciously salty and buttery popcorn, a Coke that cost seven dollars, and a bag of M&Ms the size of my face was a completely different experience from sitting on the couch with Netflix on, trying to see if I could get a slice of pizza into my mouth without pulling my arms out from under the blanket as I watched a gorgeous Hollywood actress win over the perfect man.

Especially when the last guy I'd matched with on Tinder told me on the first date that I could never come to his place of employment because he'd lied about being gay to get "diversity points" in the interview.

I really needed better taste in men.

Ryan Reynolds would never lie about being gay to get a job, I thought as I let myself enjoy the eye candy and trope-filled comedy on screen in front of me.

After about forty-five minutes, right when Emma Stone's character was starting to worry Ryan Reynolds was cheating on her, Calvin Monroe got up from his seat and snuck down the aisle toward the exit. I immediately got up and followed, along with Rosie, while Dot seemed perfectly content to sip her drink, eat her popcorn, and continue watching the movie.

For someone who pretended not to enjoy romcoms very much, she sure seemed into this one.

As we exited the theatre, it took a second for my eyes to adjust to the light, but I still managed to spot Calvin Monroe heading into the men's room halfway down the hall that led to the myriad of theatres in this Megaplex.

I checked to make sure Rosie was behind me, and the two of us headed down the hall and slipped into the men's room after him.

I was surprised at how easily Rosie had followed me in here. "I'll guard the door," she said as soon as we walked in.

Calvin Monroe—who, luckily, had been just about to undo the button on his jeans—looked at us, annoyed. "This isn't the ladies' room," he said with a scowl.

"And I don't have to pee," I replied. Wow, that sounded *incredibly* lame when said out loud. "We need to talk about James MacMahon."

"What about him? He's dead. What do you have to do with it?" Then realization dawned upon him. "You're two of those crazy idiots going for the reward money, aren't you? Get the hell out of this bathroom. Leave me alone."

"We're not leaving until you answer our questions," I said.

"Yeah, you are," Calvin said. "You can't make me answer your questions. I'm trying to enjoy a nice movie with my wife. Stop bothering me."

"We will… when you talk to us. Look, we found out where you were tonight. We know you had lunch with James MacMahon the day he was killed, and we know he screwed you out of a deal that would have been worth millions. Now, I'm pretty sure the police don't know this, because if they did, you'd have already spent a day in an interrogation room. So you can either answer our questions and then go back to your wife, confident in the knowledge that your secret is safe with us, or you can refuse to talk to us, in which case I guarantee you Jake and Liam, the two detectives working James MacMahon's case, will shortly be by to pay you a visit."

Calvin Monroe glared at me, and I returned as good as I got. Finally, after about ten seconds, he relented.

"Fine," he snapped. "You want to know what went on between James MacMahon and me? You got it. The asshole screwed me. Screwed me big time. I was supposed to be one of the major investors in his resort. I'm the one who knew all the people on the council. I introduced him to the right people. I was instrumental in getting this project off the ground. Then you know what he goes and tells me? That the company he signed the agreement under has gone bankrupt, that there's nothing left, and before they went, the last thing they did was sign over the land the resort is going on to another company in his name."

"That can't be legal," I said. "Surely."

"You're damn right it's not," Calvin said. He was practically shouting now; obviously he still took this *very* personally. "I called my lawyers that same afternoon, as soon as I left the Four Seasons. You think I was about to let him get away with this? No. Not a chance. He was going to have to pay me what he owed. But I didn't kill him. See, the instant he died, there went a good portion of my case. The only person at MacMahon's company that I dealt with was James. He was the easy one to go after at his company and the one all my contracts were signed with. Now it's going to be harder than ever to get myself back on this project.

"And you know what? I decided it's not worth it after all. That whole project is poison. I heard one of the councilmembers who backed it received death threats. I'm used to projects getting opposition from NIMBYs, but this is some next-level stuff, even for Maui. I'm out. I love money, but this is too much, even for me. They could offer me to come back onto the project, but there's no way. Death threats, and now an actual murder? I'm pissed MacMahon screwed me over, but I'm not mad I'm off that project. Can't spend all the money in the world if you're dead."

"So you're saying you didn't kill James because you don't care that he ripped you off. But you still cared before he was dead."

"I still didn't kill him. I'm telling you. I was pissed,

sure. But I've been screwed over before. I'm in property development, and it's not exactly a low-risk business. I've screwed over others, too. It's never led to anyone's death before. And I'm sure it'll happen again before I retire. But murder? That's next level."

Just then, someone tried to open the bathroom door, but Rosie had it blocked with her foot. "Sorry, closed for cleaning," Rosie said sweetly through the small gap, and whoever it was left to try another bathroom.

"Fine, where were you when James was killed?" I asked.

"What time was it?"

"Around four."

"Then I would have just gotten back from my lawyer's office. I scheduled an emergency appointment that afternoon after learning how James had screwed me."

"Can anyone vouch for you?"

Calvin shook his head. "No. I don't keep a huge office here on Maui, since most of my staff are on Oahu, and I didn't see anyone around there. I went back to Oahu in the morning. But I'm telling you, I didn't kill MacMahon."

"Do you own a knife?" I asked.

"I mean, sure. I have a kitchen, after all."

"What about a knife you'd carry around with you day to day?"

"What? No, of course not. That's ridiculous. My knives are all in my home. I don't make a habit of carrying them around with me."

"Fine. Can you think of anyone else who might want to kill James MacMahon?"

"He wasn't the most popular guy with the county councilmembers," Calvin replied with a shrug. "Also, given his roving eye, I bet his wife wants him dead, but she's in New York. Apart from that, I don't have a clue. Now, let me go. I'm telling you, I didn't kill the guy. And I'd appreciate it if you didn't get me into trouble with the cops."

"Fine. I don't like them anyway," I replied. Although I had to say, Jake was growing on me since he'd helped Zoe. Just a little bit.

Calvin shook his head as if he couldn't believe us and headed back into the hall. I supposed we had literally scared the pee out of him. Or maybe he just decided it was worth holding it to get away from us. Rosie and I followed but hung around for a minute to let him reenter the theatre first.

"What do you think?" I asked. "Killer or not?"

"He has no alibi, and he had an excellent reason to want James MacMahon dead," Rosie said. "I think he stays on the list. Plus, James would probably have taken his call."

I nodded. "Right. I agree. He's not off the list at all. It would help if we could prove he had a knife that looked like our murder weapon, though."

"I'll put Dot on it," Rosie said as we approached the theatre door. "You never know what some people like to put on the internet. Also, Dot found out today that he did, in fact, fly back to Oahu the following morning and came back again this morning. He was on the island when MacMahon was murdered."

Confident that we had a solid lead, I slipped back into the theatre with Rosie and back into our seats, settling in to enjoy the end of the movie.

"YOU KNOW WHAT THAT MOVIE NEEDED? MORE HAND grenades," Dot announced as we left the theatre.

"I'm curious as to what part of the movie would have been improved with the addition of those," I said with a smile.

"Easy. All of it. But more specifically, that scene where the abusive ex-boyfriend comes back and tries to be with her. You know what stops a man from trying to win a woman back by force? A grenade."

I laughed. "Well, I can't argue with that logic. And on that note, I have to get back home. We're going to the council meeting tomorrow?"

"We sure are," Rosie said. "Why don't we pick you up after work and head straight over from there?"

"Cool," I said. "Sounds good."

I had driven my own car—well, Zoe's car, since she and Mom had traded for a bit—to the Megaplex, so I headed straight home, where I threw some leftovers in the microwave for dinner while waiting for Zoe to come home from work.

When she did, her face was pale.

"Hey, what's wrong?" I asked, immediately heading over to her.

"He followed me from the hospital," she said, her voice barely more than a whisper. "I called 9-1-1, and I told them what was going on while I drove around in circles. I think he eventually realized what was going on, because he peeled off and went elsewhere, so by the time the cops found me, he was gone. But he was there. He followed me. They told me they would go to his place and speak with him, because he violated the TRO, but he obviously doesn't care."

"Oh, Zoe," I said, taking my friend into a big hug. She was obviously terrified. "Okay, it's time to do something about this. Something more."

"What can we do?" she asked. "What more is there? He's ignoring the restraining order."

"We catch him in the act," I replied. "Come on. We're going to spend the night at your apartment, we're going to wait for him to show up, and then we're going to strike. We're not going to wait for this creep to make his move. We're going to attack first."

"Is that even legal?" Zoe asked.

"I don't care. What he's doing isn't legal, and I'm not going to see my friend get hurt—or worse—because some creep can't take a hint."

Zoe looked uncertain. "I don't know…"

"It'll be fine," I replied. "Your mom's the best lawyer in the state. If we need someone to get us out of jail, she'll do it."

"She's a lawyer, not a miracle worker," Zoe said. "Besides, I don't want to kill anyone."

"We're not going to kill him," I replied. "We're just going to stop him so the cops can arrest him."

"This still sounds like a really bad idea."

"Have I ever steered you wrong before?"

"You tried to convince me to cheat on a test with you in tenth grade, I wouldn't do it, and you got caught, and the teacher gave you a zero."

"Okay, that's fair," I admitted. "But that was like… fifteen years ago now? And the stakes are higher here. Trust me, we'll be fine."

"That's what you said about the cheating, too," Zoe muttered. "Look, why don't we see what the police say? One of the officers called me. She said they would come by when they went to his place. If he's been arrested and he's in jail, then we don't have to worry about it. If not, then I'll consider doing things your way."

"Deal. Frankly, I hope he rots in jail here. Nothing would make me happier. But if we find out he hasn't, then I'm not going to let him ruin your life like this. You're a freaking doctor. You save people's lives every day. You shouldn't have to worry about your own because some guy never learned about boundaries."

"Thanks." Zoe took my hand and squeezed it right as a knock came at the door.

Standing at the door were two police officers. One was male, one was female. The man was native Hawaiian, while the woman was white, both standing the same way, with their fingers hooked around their utility belts. "We're looking for Zoe Morgan," the woman said.

I motioned for them to come in. "She's in the living room."

I led them in to where Zoe was still sitting on the

couch, and she gestured for the two officers to have a seat as well.

"If you don't mind, we'd like some privacy," one officer told me.

I nodded and went to the kitchen, where I opened a bag of chips and munched away for a bit before heading to my room. I played on my phone for a bit, idly checking the Facebook page for the local group on the resort development—most of the commenters were thrilled that the project was likely stalled by James MacMahon's death, but none of them seemed crazy enough that I figured they were the cause of it—until I heard the police begin to leave. I made my way back to the living room, where I found Zoe sitting on the couch, staring ahead.

"Because there's no proof he was there, they can't do anything," she said in a monotone voice, shifting her gaze to the carpet. "They were nice about it and all, but he's still out there, stalking me."

"Well, we're going to do something about it," I said.

Zoe's eyes rose to meet mine. Her jaw firmed, and she nodded. "Right. I'm with you. I've had it with feeling this way. I haven't done anything wrong, and I refuse to feel like a piece of prey waiting for the predator to strike."

"Yes," I said with a fist pump. "Let's do this."

"First, you have to promise me your plan doesn't include doing anything illegal."

"It doesn't," I said, holding my hands up as though pretending to swear on a bible. "So now he knows you're driving Mom's car, so we can't take it. Let me call a friend, who'll drive us to your place. That way we can get inside without being seen."

"Okay," Zoe said.

I sent a quick text to Rosie, and twenty minutes later, she was in front of Mom's place.

"Thanks for driving us," I said. "This is Zoe."

"Nice to meet you," Rosie said to her with a smile as Zoe shook her hand.

"You too. Thanks for the ride."

"Not a problem. Anything interesting happening tonight?"

"Zoe has a stalker, and we need to take care of it, but it means getting into her building without being seen," I replied.

"Do you need any help?"

"Thanks, but I think we've got it," I said, patting the bag I'd grabbed from the garage before we left. It held the baseball bat I'd used as a kid. I figured that was going to be all we'd need.

"Right. Well, let me know if you change your mind," Rosie said. "I can help, you know."

"Thanks, but we're okay. It's totally under control."

"Good."

Rosie drove around the block once, slowly easing past the block of apartments without stopping.

"That's him," Zoe said, her voice shaking. "He's in his car, waiting."

"Are you sure you don't want to call the cops?" Rosie asked.

Zoe nodded. "Yes. I tried that already, and they

didn't do anything. If he sees that I spotted him, he'll just leave again."

"Okay," Rosie said. "I'll drop you off at the front of the building. That way, he won't see you go in, since the parking lot is at the back."

"Good thinking," I said. "He'll have to know eventually that we're home, but I want us to get ready first."

"I have a bad feeling about this," Zoe said.

"Don't worry," I replied. "What could possibly go wrong?"

As it turned out, the answer was "so many things."

Chapter 16

I thanked Rosie for the ride, and the two of us got out of the car and darted inside. We headed to Zoe's apartment, where a bouquet of flowers had been left in front of her apartment door.

"Gross," she said, scrunching up her nose.

"We're going to take these in with us and keep them as evidence," I said. "You never know if they'll come in handy."

"Make sure he hasn't put, like, anthrax or anything in them," Zoe said.

"Oh, they're immediately going into a sealed garbage bag. Don't turn on any of the lights when you get in. I don't want him to know there's anyone here yet."

Zoe nodded, and the two of us entered her apartment. Sure enough, it was a small one bedroom, but in typical Zoe fashion, she kept it incredibly neat. The ambient light from the moon outside was just enough that I could make out the outlines of the furniture.

I headed to the kitchen and immediately grabbed a garbage bag from underneath the sink, shook it open, and dumped the flowers into it. I then sealed it up and threw the bag on the bed.

"All right, what are we doing?" Zoe asked.

"I'm going to hide. You're going to turn on the light and then close the blinds. Make sure you spend enough time in front of them that he sees you're home. Then go into the bathroom, spend about five minutes there, and then turn out all the lights, like you've gone to bed."

"We want him to know I'm here?" Zoe asked.

I nodded. "Absolutely. He won't come up if he doesn't know you're home. And we want him to come up."

"That's the last thing I want," Zoe muttered.

"Hey, better for him to come up when we're ready and waiting," I replied.

"Yeah, you're right. Okay, are you ready?"

I headed over to the couch, away from the window and certainly out of view of anyone in the parking lot. "Sure am."

Zoe flicked on the light and immediately headed to the window, closing the curtains. Then she went to the kitchen and grabbed a light snack before turning off the lights and going to the bathroom.

Meanwhile, I looked through the bag that held the bat. I figured just the threat of being hit over the head with a Louisville Slugger would be enough to scare Josh into letting himself be zip tied, and then we could deliver him to the police, signed, sealed, and delivered.

I doubted there was going to be any actual violence tonight. And oh boy, was I ever wrong.

Ten minutes later, Zoe turned off the bathroom light and came back to the living room to join me.

"You better not be planning on actually using that," she said, eyeing the baseball bat suspiciously.

"Of course not. It's just to scare him. When he knocks at the door—and I bet he will knock—we'll answer. I'll threaten to beat him with the bat if he doesn't stop stalking you, and you can zip tie his hands and feet together. Then we call the cops and wait for them to come and pick him up. We'll have the element of surprise; my bet is he'll be too surprised by being actually caught to try and run away. And if we have to, we kneecap him with the baseball bat."

"I'm not sure this was a good idea after all," Zoe said quietly. "Maybe we should just call the police."

However, at that very moment, there was a scraping sound at the door. My eyes widened as I realized what was happening.

"Holy crap," I whispered. "He isn't knocking on the door to get you to come to it. He's trying to break into your apartment."

"I think I'm going to throw up," Zoe said.

I shook my head. "No. Just make sure you have the zip ties ready. And maybe call 9-1-1 right now."

Zoe nodded and pulled out her phone, dialing the number. The scraping sounds from outside seemed to be getting louder. This was way worse than just some guy who couldn't take no for an answer.

Part of me wanted to panic, to freak out. I had

planned on just threatening the guy outside the door with a baseball bat, maybe scaring him to the point that he would pee himself. But now that he was trying to enter Zoe's apartment, I knew things were a lot worse. He might be armed. It was possible he had a knife—or a gun.

But I also knew that panicking would only lead to me dying. Much like when I had faced off against that idiot in the jewelry store in Seattle, I had to keep my wits about me. That would give Zoe and me the best chance to get out of here unharmed.

As soon as Josh entered the apartment, he would be in the dark. He probably wouldn't want to turn the lights on straight away to avoid detection for as long as possible. I snuck forward while Zoe whispered what was going on into the phone to the emergency operator, and I grabbed as many pairs of her shoes as I could find.

Luckily, shoes had always been Zoe's only vanity-based passion. Growing up, she had been all about minimal makeup, and her fashion sense was always stylish but all about function. Shoes, on the other hand... she had at least half a dozen pairs in the open closet by the door. I spread them out on the floor as quietly as I could. If I was lucky, Josh would trip on them as soon as he came in.

Stepping back, I grabbed the bat and held it at the ready. If I had to bust a few kneecaps, well, that was what he got for trying to break into my friend's apartment.

Zoe hung up the phone and whispered in my ear.

"The police are on their way. They should be here soon."

At that exact moment, the lock on the door clicked. "Looks like not soon enough," I whispered back. "Get ready."

I pressed myself against the wall of the living room so that when Josh opened the door, the light pouring in from the hallway wouldn't immediately betray our presence. That was when I realized it *would* allow him to see the shoes I'd spread out to trap him.

Shoot. Well, it was too late to do anything about it now.

The door opened, and the tiniest gasp escaped Zoe's lips next to me.

"Well, well," a man's voice said quietly. "It looks like you need lessons in keeping your shoes a bit tidier, my Nubian queen."

Nubian queen? Barf. Why did some dudes have to be so *creepy*?

He closed the door carefully behind him and stepped over the shoes, inching his way toward the living room, where I was still pressed against the wall.

The element of surprise was the biggest advantage I had right now—well, and the baseball bat—and I was going to use it to my full advantage.

I listened as Josh's footsteps got closer, and when he was only about a foot away from me, I struck.

I spun out away from the wall and swung the bat directly at his midsection. My hit was direct, and he let out a howl of pain as he collapsed against the wall.

"Zoe, now," I called out, and she arrived with the zip ties.

But before she managed to get them around his wrists, Josh pushed away from the wall and tackled her.

"Stupid whore," he shouted.

As Zoe let out a scream, I threw on the lights to see better, just in time to see Zoe kick Josh right between the legs. He let out another yelp, and that was when he pulled out a knife. It had been in his pocket, and he pressed the button to flick the blade open.

"No!" I shouted, bringing the baseball bat down on his hand. The knife clattered to the ground, and I kicked it toward the living room as hard as I could. Then adrenaline took over, and I hit him right in the knees. There came a sickening crack, and he screamed before falling to the ground.

The zip ties had spread out all over the floor, so I reached down and grabbed the closest one, forcing Josh's hands together as I tied them tight.

"What are you doing?" he shouted. "You broke my kneecap! You fucking bitch, you broke my kneecap!"

"I wish I had sedatives here at home," Zoe muttered. She joined me, tying Josh's feet together.

He continued to shout and curse at us for about five minutes until the police arrived, guns drawn. They were the same two officers that had come by Mom's house earlier tonight.

As soon as they saw Zoe and me and the shape Josh was in, they holstered their weapons.

"What happened here?" the woman asked. "I thought you were staying at her mother's house."

"That was the plan, but Zoe didn't have any clothes, and she was missing some stuff she needed for work tomorrow," I chimed in quickly.

Zoe nodded. "We were only supposed to be here five minutes. But he broke in just a couple minutes after we'd come in here. Luckily, we had time to get my baseball bat and some zip ties."

"Liar!" Josh screamed. "You're a liar!"

"Get him out of here," the woman said to her partner.

The male officer dragged Josh to his feet, cuffed him over the zip ties, and dragged him out of the apartment, with Josh howling that I'd broken his kneecap with every fresh step.

"*Now* are you taking him to jail?" Zoe asked the woman.

She nodded. "Yes. We're going to need a statement from both of you."

"That's fine," I said. "As long as he's locked up."

"After what I've seen tonight, I have to say he's probably going to enjoy a nice stint at Halawa."

I nodded, reaching over and squeezing Zoe's hand. I knew this nightmare wasn't over yet. If Josh decided to go to court or otherwise try and draw things out, Zoe was going to have to face him in court. But I knew if anyone could handle it, she could.

"You're very lucky, you know," the woman told her.

"She wouldn't have had to be lucky if he'd been locked up the first time she called," I pointed out. "We already knew he was dangerous."

"I know," the female officer said, pressing her lips

together. "There was nothing we could do about that, though. Legally, our hands were tied."

"Well, now his hands are tied," I said with a grin, unable to resist the jest.

"Seriously? Now?" Zoe asked me.

I shrugged. "The opening was there. Sometimes you just have to take your shot."

The female officer continued as if I hadn't said anything. "All right. Do you want to come down to the station now to give your statements?"

"That's probably best—get it over with," I said, looking over at Zoe.

She nodded. "I agree. I don't think I'm going to be getting much sleep tonight anyway."

My phone binged, indicating that I'd received a text. I checked it to find it was from Rosie, just a thumbs-up.

I smiled to myself and then was gripped with panic. We didn't have a car here. Rosie had dropped us off. I texted her quickly. *We need to borrow your car.*

No problem.

Relief washed over me instantly. Since we'd told the officer that we were just stopping by for five minutes, it made no sense for us not to have a ride.

"We'll meet you at the station," I said to the woman.

She nodded. "You know how to get there?"

"You're right off the Piilani Highway, right?"

"That's the one. I'll see you soon."

The woman headed after her partner, and I turned to Zoe. "Are you okay?"

"Yeah. Are you?"

I nodded. "Yeah. I'm with you about not getting too much sleep tonight, though."

We walked down the hallway together, and Zoe whispered, her voice quavering slightly, "I can't believe he broke into my home."

"You can stay with Mom and me for as long as you need," I told her.

Zoe smiled. "Thanks. I might have to take you up on that, actually. I'm just… I'm not sure I can stay in that apartment again. At least, not yet. Even if he is in jail."

I nodded. "Of course."

We headed back out via the front door and spotted Rosie's car parked a little ways down the street, engine idling. Zoe slipped into the passenger seat while I climbed in the back.

"I saw him being taken away in cuffs," Rosie said. "I figured I'd hang around for a while just in case. How did it go?"

"He broke into the apartment," I replied. "Actually fully broke in. He tried to attack us. He had a knife, but it turns out my baseball bat was better."

"Good. He was limping pretty badly and shouting, although I couldn't make out the words. But I can give you the gist of it," Rosie said with a small smile. "Now, you need the car?"

I nodded. "We told the police we were here to pick up some things for Zoe. It would be weird for us not to have taken it. And now we have to go meet them at the station."

"That's fine with me. You can drop me off at Dot's."

"Are you sure?" I asked. "We can always stop off at your place first."

Rosie shook her head. "No, no, that's all right. Dot is still awake, anyway. Drop me off at her place, and you can feel free to take the car."

"All right," I said as Rosie pulled away from the corner.

A couple minutes later, we were at Dot's place, and I took the keys from Rosie, taking her spot in the driver's seat as she leaned through the window to say goodbye. "I'll drop these off tomorrow before work."

"Thank you, Charlie. And I am glad you're both all right."

"Me too," I replied with a grim face. "It was kind of touch and go for a minute there."

"I'll get Dorothy to see what she can dig up on the man. Do you know his name?"

"Josh Newman," I replied.

Rosie nodded. "Good. If there's anything in his past that will help, I'll make sure the cops get it."

I thanked Rosie again, and Zoe and I headed silently toward the police station.

Chapter 17

Before we got there, Zoe and I went over our story a couple of times. It wasn't as if there was a lot to get sorted out. After all, most of our story was true. But we had to make sure there were no discrepancies at all.

"I really hope this doesn't go to court," Zoe said. "I don't want to lie on the stand. We shouldn't have lied in the first place. We should have just told the truth. After all, there's nothing illegal about what we did."

I shook my head. "No way. You saw what happened the first time around. The system is not designed to reward people who try and stop crimes from happening to them. We'll stick with our story for now, and we'll burn that bridge when we get to it, if we get to it."

"That's not really the expression," Zoe said with a chuckle.

"I know what I said.

"Maybe you're right."

"I am right. Of the two of us, I have much more

experience with lying, so I know the consequences of it much better."

Zoe laughed. "I can't argue with that."

"It'll be fine, I promise."

Sure enough, the two of us went in and gave our statement. The police officer didn't even bother separating us, so we were able to hear everything the other said and corroborate each other's stories without difficulty.

"Thank you for coming in so late," the woman told us when we left. "I've got your contact information, Zoe, so I'll be in touch."

By the time we left the station, it was well after midnight, and the air had cooled down to about sixty degrees. It was still warm enough that I didn't need a jacket, but the breeze had the slightest edge to it, warning that winter was on its way.

Of course, compared to what the weather was like in Seattle right now, this was downright balmy.

Zoe and I drove home mostly in silence, each of us wrapped in her own thoughts.

"You know he's not getting out of jail anytime soon, right?" I asked Zoe, looking at her out of the corner of my eye. She'd been staring out the passenger-side window, looking up at the stars.

"I hope not," Zoe muttered. "I can't believe it. I've never felt this unsafe in my life. What can you do when someone is literally stalking you and trying to attack you? I mean, I'm glad he's behind bars, but that's insane. I can't describe the fear I'm going through right now."

"I actually know exactly what it feels like," I said quietly.

Zoe looked over at me. "Of course you do. I completely forgot that this is the same sort of thing that drove you to Hawaii."

"If you want to move to Seattle for a while, until he's locked up permanently, I'd understand," I said with a grin.

Zoe laughed. "You know, it's actually tempting. But I love my job, and I don't want to leave it. And I love this island. No, I'm not going to let him drive me away from here, especially now that he's in jail and unlikely to get out anytime soon. But I completely understand why you did what you did, coming back to somewhere that's so painful just to get away."

I nodded. "Yeah. When a human finger was left on my doorstep... I mean, I like to think I can handle myself, but that was just a whole other level."

"No kidding. I saw you with that baseball bat. You can unquestionably take care of yourself. But when your life is threatened, and you spend every waking moment wondering if it's going to be your last, things are different."

"Exactly."

WE DROVE IN SILENCE FOR THE REST OF THE RIDE before pulling up in front of the house once more. Mom was still awake, sitting on the couch, watching TV.

"Are you girls all right?" she asked.

I nodded. "Did you stay up just to check on us?"

"No, of course not. I just couldn't sleep, so I figured I'd watch some TV with Coco here, who seems to appreciate the company."

I smiled. I had a sneaking suspicion Mom was lying, but I wasn't going to call her out on it. As much as she could be frustrating at times—the comment to Jake about handcuffs was going to mortify me to my dying day—I knew she loved me more than anything in the world. And I was eternally grateful to her for taking me in now, especially after I'd run away from Hawaii as fast as I could after Dad's death and sworn that I'd never come back.

"Well, it's all sorted out," I said. "You don't have to worry about us. Zoe's stalker is in jail, and he's not getting out anytime soon."

"I'm happy to hear that," Mom said, stifling a yawn. "Well, would you look at that? Maybe I'm a bit more tired than I thought I was. Good night, girls."

"Good night."

And with that, Mom got up from her spot on the couch and headed to her room. I knew she had been lying. She had totally had stayed up to wait for us.

"I'll see you in the morning," I said to Zoe.

"Yeah. Thanks again."

SURE ENOUGH, A MIXTURE OF ADRENALINE AND STRESS —not the world's best emotional combination—meant I spent most of the night tossing and turning, and when I got to work the next day, I went straight for a scoop of espresso ice cream.

"You know, as much as I'd like to encourage the adoption of ice cream as a three-meal-a-day kind of food, I feel as though I should point out that there exist other options," Leslie said to me when I finished making my milkshake and poured it into a glass. "Options that might, as much as it pains me to say it, be a little bit healthier for you."

"I know, but I had to drop a car off at a friend's place this morning and walk here from there, and I'm not an organized enough human to both do that *and* get up in time to make a healthy breakfast."

"Well, the first step to fixing a problem is recognizing it," Leslie said with a chuckle. "You look like you need that espresso, anyway. Are you not getting enough sleep?"

I shook my head and explained to her what had happened.

When I was finished, Leslie swore under her breath. "I'm glad you're all right. If you want to go home early to crash, just let me know. I'm sure I can handle one day here by myself."

"Thanks," I said gratefully. "I think I'll probably be able to power through, though."

When I was twenty-one or twenty-two years old, I could easily spend an entire night chugging down as much alcohol as my liver could safely process, really testing the limits of that whole metabolization thing, then go to work the next day feeling a little under the weather but nothing that a few greasy McDonald's hash browns and some Gatorade couldn't fix.

Now that I was in my late twenties, though, things were a bit different. I spent the whole day feeling like I'd been hit by a truck. Every muscle in my body hurt, and I hadn't even been drinking at all. This wasn't fair; getting old sucked.

Still, I stuck it out, and when I finally said bye to Leslie around three, I realized I had virtually no memory of having served any customers. I'd just spent the entire day on autopilot. And that was when I remembered I had said I'd go to the Maui council meeting with Rosie and Dot.

I groaned as I started walking home, trying to figure out if I should ask Mom to come pick me up. After all, Zoe's shift at the hospital started at noon, so she wouldn't be around. But I'd just barely left the ice cream shop when a car pulled up next to me, and Rosie waved me in. That was right; they were going to pick me up after my shift. I really *was* tired.

"Come on."

I slipped into the backseat. Dot was driving, focusing intently on the road.

"How are you feeling after last night?"

"Honestly? I didn't get any sleep, I'm functioning entirely on two espresso milkshakes, and I'm kind of hoping Dot drives this car straight into the ocean and finishes me off."

Dot laughed. "So, a good day then. Why don't you lie down in the back? We'll wake you up when we get there."

"A twenty-minute nap is a perfect rejuvenator," Rosie added. "Physiologically, your body will feel refreshed and healthy, whereas if you sleep for a shorter or longer period of time—up until the next full sleep cycle of ninety minutes—you'll be groggy. So go ahead and sleep. We'll wake you up, and you'll feel much better."

I murmured my thanks and closed my eyes. I was fairly sure I was asleep in seconds.

Chapter 18

"Charlie, wake up," Dot said, shaking my leg.

I moaned and kicked at her slightly.

"We're here," Rosie said. "The meeting's going to start in a few minutes."

I blinked myself awake and found that to my surprise, I was actually fairly alert.

"I let you sleep for exactly twenty minutes," Rosie said. "We've been in the parking lot for five. Ready to go?"

"I am, actually. Thanks." I was surprised at how energetic I felt. Maybe there was something to this whole twenty-minute-nap thing after all.

We were in Wailuku, at the Kalana O Maui building, where council meetings were held. Obviously built in the era when concrete was cheap and aesthetics were not an architectural priority, the approximately ten-story building dominated the landscape on this part of the island. I followed Dot and Rosie as we made our way to the eighth floor, where the meeting would take place.

The inside of the chamber was set up in the same way as most other local meeting places. Wooden desks at the front had spots for all of the councilmembers, while a few rows of cushioned bench-style seating offered plenty of space for onlookers to come by and watch proceedings.

As I looked around, I had to admit there were more people here than I had expected. I even spotted Charles Buchanan sitting himself down at the end of one of the rows, supporting himself with his hands on his knees as he lowered his rear. He breathed out a sigh and looked around, and as soon as he spotted me, he glared.

Apparently there were hard feelings from the other day at Starbucks after all. I flashed him a smile and a finger wave, and he replied with a rude gesture. I snickered to myself before turning to my two companions.

Before I had a chance to say anything, however, the councilmembers filed in.

"All right, fill me in on who's who that we suspect might be the killer," I whispered to Rosie, who was sitting next to me.

"The woman at the seat at the end there is Janice Evers," Rosie whispered back, her lips barely moving.

I followed her eyes to see a rather portly woman with curly white hair that framed a friendly-looking face wearing rose-rimmed glasses that didn't suit her in the least. Her suit looked like it was from the eighties, complete with shoulder pads. But she chose that moment to look up from her papers and look around the room. As she smiled at the attendees, I understood her charisma; she looked fresh and energetic and suddenly about fifteen years younger when she interacted with the crowd.

"She's retiring at the end of this term, so she doesn't need to worry about her re-election," Rosie continued. "Next to her is Natalie Lee. She also voted for the project to go ahead. She was so unpopular, even before this vote, that everyone knows she doesn't have a snowball's chance of being re-elected, so she might have decided to cash out while she still had a bit of power and influence."

I looked over to see a woman who might have been half Chinese, half Hawaiian. Her tawny skin was flawless, and her black hair was tied back into a neat ponytail. Her black eyes ran over something she had written in the notebook in front of her. The man seated next to her leaned over and whispered something into her ear. She scoffed and shook her head, obviously annoyed by whatever he'd just said to her.

"And Albert Millner?" I asked.

Rosie pointed discreetly to a man sitting two chairs down from Natalie. He looked like every other politician, with a blindingly white smile, a haircut that probably cost more than my rent back in Seattle, and a perfectly tailored suit. He occasionally looked up and flashed a smile to the crowd before going back to texting on his phone.

"I'm surprised he voted for the project, really. He's popular, and he could have a long career in front of him. I wouldn't be surprised if he tries to move into state politics soon. If I had to guess, I'd say he took bribe money, knowing that the next election is eighteen months away and thinking that he could win back the voters before then, that they'd have long forgotten about the project by that point."

Before I had a chance to reply, the council meeting was called to order, and I very quickly decided that if I ever needed help falling asleep again, I'd just have to play a recording of one of these things.

First, the minutes from the previous meeting were read out. Then, they went through the business for the current meeting. Did it really take forty-five minutes to discuss whether or not a certain intersection needed a four-way stop or a traffic light? And then they didn't even come to a final decision. Things didn't actually get interesting until the floor was opened for questions from the public, and it took nearly ninety minutes to get to that point.

As soon as the floor was opened for questions, Charles stood up.

"Yes, Charles?" one of the councilmembers I didn't recognize said with a sigh. Obviously, this wasn't his first attendance at one of these meetings.

"I'd like to know what's going to happen to the Kinolio Resort now that the man heading up the company in charge of the project has been murdered."

"Well, as far as this council is concerned, nothing has changed," Natalie replied, leaning forward slightly as she answered the question. "Permission to build the hotel wasn't given to James MacMahon specifically; it was given to MacMahon Developments Incorporated. So long as the company still exists, it has permission to continue building."

A murmur of disapproval spread through the room. Obviously, this wasn't the answer people had been hoping for.

"I want to know if you still get your payoff from the company now that he's dead. Or did you get paid in advance?" Charlie shouted.

"All right, that's enough," Natalie snapped. "If you can't control yourself, I'll have security escort you out."

"That's right, try and stifle my right to free speech," Charles shouted. "You're a sellout. You and your two friends over there. You'll go down in history as this island's Judas, selling Kihei for thirty pieces of silver."

"Okay, that's enough. I'm calling security," Natalie said, her eyes flashing as she pulled out her phone.

"He's right, though," a woman called out from the other side of the room. "You did sell us out. And now the man in charge of the project is dead, and you're saying there's nothing you can do to stop it going forward? You belong in jail, every last one of you."

"That's enough," the man in the middle seat said. His voice was calm but authoritative. This was Jeremy Kenochi, the mayor of Maui. "I'll remind everyone here that it's a privilege to sit in on these meetings, not a right. If you can't control yourselves, you'll be asked to leave."

"Yeah, and it's a privilege that you get to serve us," Charles replied. "But right now, three of the people up there aren't doing that at all. They took cash instead of doing what was right for the community and the people they were elected to serve."

"An investigation was opened, and there was no evidence of any wrongdoing by any of the members of the council," Kenochi said.

"Oh, yeah, I'm sure you looked *real* hard for it," Charlie snapped as a couple of men in brown uniforms entered the room.

Natalie pointed out Charlie, and the two men headed right for him, their expressions serious.

"That's right. Kick me out. It's easier than addressing the real issue here: that half this council is corrupt. You can get rid of me, but you can't get rid of what I'm talking about. Everyone in this crowd knows I have a point."

"He does," the woman who had spoken up earlier said. "This resort is bad news for Kihei and bad news for this island as a whole. No one believes the three councilors who voted for the development did so because they genuinely thought it was a good idea. This is your chance to make it right."

"As has already been stated," Kenochi repeated, "there's nothing we can do now as council. The resolution was passed to allow Kinolio Resort to be built. If the company is still willing to build the resort on the land it purchased, then that's that. I recommend you petition management to change its mind on the project, but given what it's already invested to make it work, I find it unlikely that they're going to be open to it."

"Yeah, invested directly into your pockets," Charlie snapped as the two security guards approached him.

"Sir, come with us, please," one of the guards said. He looked like a Coke machine with eyes, weighing at least two hundred and fifty pounds, with a couple of beady black eyes set deep in his thick skull.

"I will not," Charlie snapped, yanking his arm away from the guard and taking a few steps to the side.

"Sir," the other guard said, his voice full of warning, "this is private property, and you've been asked to leave. You have no choice."

"Well, this might get interesting," Rosie muttered into my ear.

I nodded, transfixed by the scene in front of us.

Charlie looked at the two men, and when Mr. Coke Machine stepped forward, Charlie leapt up and jumped onto the bench in front of him.

"You can't take my free speech! These people are criminals! They're the ones you should be kicking out of here. Not me! I'll fight to the death on this."

Charlie began running down the aisle as the two security guards chased him.

Squeals and yelps emanated from the crowd as people tried to get out of the way of the slow-moving chase. Of course, this wasn't exactly the Ritz, so the benches were close enough together that in order to get by people, Charlie had to squeeze past their legs, and so did the security guards going after him.

Given that none of the three were exactly small human beings, it ended up being a kind of slow-motion chase as all of them tried to scurry past the people on the benches.

Eventually, Charlie jumped over the other railing leading toward the councilors.

"Out, out," Kenochi ordered, and all five of them immediately rushed out the side door.

"I'm not finished with you! You're taking our futures! This can't continue!" Charlie shouted as the councilors all quickly scuttled out of the room. Albert Millner looked behind him at one point, the fear in his eyes obvious.

As Charlie rushed toward them, that was when the security guards had reached their limit. Mr. Coke Machine pulled out a gun and pointed it at Charlie. "That's enough! Get on the ground now!" he roared.

Even Charlie Buchanan wasn't dumb enough to keep going with a gun pointed at his chest. He stopped and glared at the security guards, but sure enough, he put his hands up and dropped to his knees.

"The police are on their way," the second security guard informed him. "I don't want to see you move until they get here. Everybody else, out."

"I kind of want to stay and see if they shoot him," Dot murmured as we got up with everyone else and headed out.

"I have to go to the bathroom," I said as I spotted a sign indicating the ladies' room down the hall. "Is it all right if I meet you back at the car?"

"Of course," Dot replied. "The thing is, I've been looking into those councilors as well, and I can't find how James MacMahon might have bribed them. All of their bank accounts look completely spotless."

"Maybe Charlie is wrong about it?" I suggested.

"It's possible, but I doubt it. There's no reason for the councilmembers to have voted in favor of the development otherwise. Well, apart from blackmail. I'll keep looking when I get home."

"Okay," I said. "I'll meet you back at the car.

Chapter 19

I followed the sign to the other end of the hallway, where I found the women's bathroom. Slipping into the stall at the end, I did my business while thinking over what we'd just seen.

Charlie Buchanan was angry, but we already knew that. There were many reasons I didn't think he was our killer, and all of them were still valid. He wasn't a planner. He wouldn't have had James MacMahon's number to text him. And even if he had, I doubted James would have stopped for him. Certainly not when he was in that much of a rush.

I wondered also about the councilmembers. Sure, there had been an investigation. And Dot hadn't found anything. She seemed to be pretty good with computers, but was she *that* good? I mean, she had a nice setup and all, but she was still a septuagenarian retired librarian. It wasn't as if she was Edward Snowden.

The door to the bathroom creaked open, and I

didn't think anything of it until a moment later, when two women began talking.

"He's making waves, Janice." It was the voice of Natalie Lee, one of the councilmembers. She was obviously speaking to one of her coworkers.

I instinctively lifted my feet off the floor, hiding them from view so that the women wouldn't realize they weren't alone in the bathroom.

"So what? He's always made waves. It's not like this is the first time we're dealing with someone like him, and it's not the first time we're dealing with these accusations."

Natalie sighed. "I know, but it's just bringing everything back to the forefront. Look, I just don't like having this much pressure on me."

"Well, that's what you signed up for. Did you think this was going to be easy? Did you think we weren't going to face any pressure for the decision we made?"

One of the taps turned on.

"Of course not. I knew we were going to catch some flak for it, but I figured it would have been over by now."

"It is over. The investigation didn't find anything, as MacMahon said it wouldn't. You've got your number for the overseas account. Now all you have to do is wait out the rest of your term. You're going to lose your bid for re-election, and you can go about your life," Janice Evers said. "You planned on moving to the Big Island, right? That money will buy you a nice house in Hilo, or wherever on the island you want to go, and you can live in anonymity from there.

"That's my plan. My daughter lives in Kona and is having my first grandchild next year. I plan on moving there and living my best life."

"Exactly. I'm doing the same, but I'm moving to Oahu. I've spent years on this island, listening to idiots complain that they want a stop sign on their street, and this is my reward."

"That's if we don't get caught first."

"You keep your mouth shut, and we won't," Janice said sharply. "That's what all of this hinges on: everyone keeping their mouth shut. MacMahon is dead, so he can't admit to anything anymore. And if I know men like him, he didn't tell a lot of people at his company what was going on. It was all need to know, because plausible deniability is key in situations like this."

"And Albert? He'll be quiet?"

"Of course he will. Albert's a professional. He knows what this is all about." Janice's voice was quietly confident.

"This isn't the first time you've done this, is it?" Natalie asked, and I could practically *feel* Janice smiling through the stall doors.

"Honey, remember what I said about plausible deniability? You're young, you're not a career politician, and frankly, I think it's good for you that you took this offer and torched your career. You can find something else to do on the Big Island. No one will ever think twice of it, and you'll have come out of it a million bucks richer."

So, a million dollars each—that had been the payoff MacMahon handed the three councilors to get their vote. I would have let out a low whistle if it hadn't meant I would get caught eavesdropping.

"You don't think we're in any real danger, do you?" Natalie asked. "What if Charlie is the one who killed MacMahon? What if he did it to stop the project, and now that it isn't going ahead, he's going to kill us, too?" Natalie's voice had risen an octave. She was obviously panicking.

"Okay, you need to get it together," Janice said firmly. "None of that's going to happen. The police have it all under control. Whoever killed MacMahon killed him, and no one else. You should tell the police that you're worried for your safety when they get here, and they'll park a car outside your house. It'll be fine. Besides, Charlie's being arrested. He's not going to kill you."

"You can't know that for sure."

"I do. And beyond that, I know that panicking isn't going to do anyone any good. All you're going to do by panicking is say something dumb. And trust me: if you go out and do something stupid that leads to all of us getting caught, I *will* make sure you pay."

Damn. Janice might have looked like a kindly older woman, but she was *not* messing around. There was silence from Natalie for a moment.

"Come on. Wash your face, and we're going to go out and face the police," Janice said, her voice sounding a bit gentler this time. "Tell them you're worried about your safety, and they'll take care of you. And I promise you, there's nothing to worry about."

"I still can't believe MacMahon is dead," Natalie said. A moment later I heard the splashing of water, indicating that she was obeying Janice's instructions. "I mean, he seemed nice."

"Of course he seemed nice," Janice said, her voice frigid. "All men like that seem nice. They plaster on a smile, and they're charming and friendly, and it hides the fact that deep down, they'd stab you in the throat for a bit of money while they play grab-ass with their secretaries as they leave their wives at home. MacMahon wasn't a nice guy. He was a guy who wanted something and was willing to pay for it. Goodness, you really are too naïve for politics. What did you say you did before this?"

"I was a kindergarten teacher," Natalie replied.

"Why on earth did you go into politics?" Janice asked, obviously taken aback.

"I wanted to make a difference," Natalie replied, defiance in her voice. "I wanted to make this island a better place. And I quickly discovered that politics was not the way to do it."

"Oh, sweet summer child," Janice said, clucking her tongue. "You were certainly wrong about that. At least you found out the truth quickly and were willing to cash out. Listen. Use your money for something good."

"I will. When I move to Kona, I plan on helping out at the animal shelter."

"Great. That's a fantastic plan. Now come on, let's go."

The door swung open, and a moment later, I heard

it close again. I sighed out a breath I didn't even realize I'd been holding, then my eyes widened. Holy crap. I'd just heard Natalie and Janice admit they'd been bribed! At the very least, we at least knew that had happened. Natalie, Janice, and Albert had each taken a million dollars from James MacMahon in order to approve the development.

How the investigation had failed to find anything was beyond me, but then again, I had a sneaking suspicion it wasn't the first time MacMahon had done that sort of thing. He probably had a whole team of lawyers on retainer who knew exactly how to hide that kind of payoff.

I decided to wait another minute before leaving the bathroom. I didn't want to be caught leaving only seconds after Janice and Natalie; if they were still in the hallway, they'd see me.

I stood at the sink, idly running my fingers through my hair. It turned out the short nap I'd had in the back of Dot's car had made me look a little bit like the lion from *The Wizard of Oz*. Great. I was so much more of a Glinda.

I muttered under my breath about how Rosie or Dot could have told me I looked like the victim in a horror movie when the bathroom door opened, and in walked a woman about my age, her eyes looking around furtively. She was about five-ten, with curly dark hair, and had muscles that made Madonna look like a limp noodle. Dressed in a tank top and jeans, she was obviously no-nonsense.

"You!" she said. "Were you in here a moment ago?"

"No," I lied. "I just came in here."

The woman narrowed her coal-black eyes at me. "I don't believe you. You were in here when the two councilwomen were talking, weren't you?"

"Sorry, I don't know what you're talking about." I tried to keep my voice level, working hard to pull off the lie believably, but the pounding in my chest was bound to give me away. I had no idea who this woman was, but I wasn't about to tell her anything about what I'd overheard.

"Don't lie to me," the woman hissed, coming closer. "What will it take to tell me what they said? Did they admit to taking bribes? Did one of them tell you she killed James MacMahon?"

Realization dawned on me. "You're trying to find his killer."

"You're damn right I am. I'm a private investigator here on Maui, and I'm going to find the murderer."

"And pick up a tidy hundred grand for doing it."

"If you have any information that can help me, I'll make it worth your while. I treat my informants *very* well."

"Sorry," I said with a shrug. "I really don't know anything that can help you. But I hope you find the person who killed that guy. I don't like walking around knowing there's a murderer on the streets."

"I don't believe you," the woman said, placing her hands on her hips.

"Well, you got me. All you needed to do was accuse me of lying *just* the right number of times, and I now can give it all up to you. Yeah, the councilwomen were in here, and they were both gossiping about how they murdered MacMahon and dumped his body in the ocean."

"Are you serious?"

"No, of course I'm not. I've already told you, I don't know squat. Now, if you'll excuse me, bathrooms are for peeing in, not for chatting."

I seriously had to stop trying to sound cool and badass in the middle of bathrooms. It never worked.

I stepped past the woman, and she pulled a card from her pocket, holding it out to me. "Seriously. If you change your mind or find out anything, let me know. I'll take care of you."

I rolled my eyes, took the card, and walked out of the bathroom. I had briefly considered making a show of crumpling the card or maybe tearing it up and dropping the pieces in front of her just to show the woman how serious I was about not helping her. But I figured the card would at least give me a name in case I had to watch out for her again.

After all, we were both on the same track to find the killer, and I wanted that hundred grand for me, Dot, and Rosie. I wasn't about to let some private investigator who thought she was hot stuff get in there ahead of us.

Taking the elevator back down to the ground floor, I looked at the card. Alicia Gilmore, private investigator. Her contact information was listed below.

When I reached the front of the building a moment later, Dot and Rosie were idling out front.

"What were you doing in there, giving drugs to a racehorse?"

"What? No. How would I even get a… you know what, never mind. Listen, you're never going to believe what just happened."

Chapter 20

"I wonder where they're hiding the money," Dot mused. "I haven't been able to find a trace of it."

"Well, I'm sure they're not just posting pictures on Instagram of their bank account details," I replied.

Dot turned around. "Excuse me, young lady, but I've hacked into government departments you don't even know exist."

"Sorry," I said, holding up my hands.

Still, it was obvious why Dot hadn't found the accounts. They were hidden in some sort of offshore bank that wasn't public knowledge. If the investigators couldn't find the money, there was no way Dot was going to manage it.

"It certainly gives the three of them a motive," Rosie mused quietly, almost to herself. "What if one of them decided they had to get rid of the person who paid them off?"

"I can't imagine it being Natalie," I said. "She looked confident and sure of herself at the meeting, but the reality is she's scared as hell. She's worried that whoever killed James is going to come after the councilmembers next. So that tells me she didn't do it."

"Unless she was lying to make herself look less guilty," Dot pointed out.

"Sure, but why bother lying to just Janice? It's not like the two detectives were in the room with them."

"No, but Janice telling her to ask the police for protection gives her the perfect backstory to look more innocent," Rosie pointed out. "I agree that we can't rule out Natalie just because she *seems* scared. And she might have been a teacher to begin with, but that doesn't mean she's not a killer."

"I can see the moniker now: The Kindergarten Killer," I said, running my hands across the blank space in front of me as if tracing a headline. "But you're right, I guess. I shouldn't rule her out just because of that. And then there's Albert. He wasn't involved in the conversation for obvious reasons, but it sounded as though he had also been bribed."

"I wish they'd mentioned a little bit more about the details of the bribe," Dot muttered almost to herself. "Where are they hiding that money that I can't find it?"

"It doesn't even matter, really," Rosie said. "Sure, it would affect municipal politics, but the fact that I know the money was transferred is really all we need. The three councilmembers were bribed. That's a fact we're aware of now. Did one of them decide for some reason to kill MacMahon? To hide the proof of the bribery or for some other reason?"

I sighed as I leaned my head against the seat and

closed my eyes. "Why did the guy have so many people with potential reasons to kill him? Couldn't we have gotten some easier case to solve for a load of reward money?"

"That's the problem with your generation: you're always looking for the easy way out, whether it be participation trophies or an easy murder case to solve," Dot said.

"Hey, yours is the generation that handed out those trophies. No one had a gun to your head saying it was necessary," I pointed out.

"Can we not do this here?" Rosie asked. "Now, tell us about the private investigator."

"Oh, yeah. She was weird. I don't know what to tell you beyond what I've already mentioned. She offered me money in exchange for telling her what had happened in the bathroom."

"Did you take it?" Dot asked.

I shook my head. "Of course not."

"Too bad. You should have taken it then lied to her."

I swore under my breath. Damn it. Why hadn't I thought of that?

Dot grinned as her eyes met mine in the rearview mirror. "Next time."

"Yeah, thanks for the tip. I don't know what she knows. She was pretty aggressive."

"We can't worry about what the other people trying to solve this case are doing," Rosie pointed out. "The only thing we can do is our best to find the killer. Focusing on other people and how far along they are only takes our focus away from this case. I was just wondering if she might have said anything that could have been a hint that might lead us to the killer. Maybe she let something slip inadvertently."

I thought back to the conversation and shook my head slowly. "No, I don't think so. She was the one trying to get information out of me, not the other way around."

"Well, that's too bad. Because frankly, at the moment, I'm not sure what our next step is," Rosie said. "Do either one of you have any idea?"

The voice of Harry Styles crooning his latest hit through the radio was the only sound in reply.

"Great," Dot said. "So we're out of ideas, we have too many suspects, and we have nowhere to go from here."

"Well when you put it that way, it sounds impossible," I replied.

"Just because we don't have an immediate answer doesn't mean we're never going to come up with anything," Rosie said. "Let's take a day or two away from the case. You never know what will happen when you take a bit of a break and let your brain relax a little."

"Sure," I replied. "That sounds good. I'm not working the next few days anyway."

"I'm okay with that too," Dot said. "I have some stuff I want to look at that's unrelated as well, which will take some time."

Agreeing to take a few days away from the case, Rosie and Dot dropped me off at home once more, and I entered the house, wondering how Zoe's day had gone.

She was sitting at the dining table with my mom, the two of them sipping wine while playing Scrabble.

"Charlie," Zoe said warmly when she saw me. "Come join us. We only just started, so you're not losing by too much. Yet."

I laughed as I grabbed a glass from the kitchen and sat down next to my best friend. "You should give us both a head start in points just to make it a bit more fair. Otherwise you're going to crush us both."

"Hey, I can hold my own in a game of Scrabble just fine," Mom pointed out.

"Sure, but you've never played Zoe. She's a master at this. Seriously, Mom. I used to lose to her by hundreds of points back in high school."

"I don't know about that," Mom said. "I used to beat you, too."

"Yeah, when I was eight."

I selected a random set of pieces and looked at the board. Sure enough, they'd only played a couple of words so far, and I was easily able to make "cower" out of an "o" that was already on the board.

Mom wrote down my score while nodding approvingly. "Not too bad for a first play. You are better at this than when you were eight."

"My vocabulary improved slightly," I offered.

Mom smiled. "Yeah, you learned more swear words."

I laughed as Zoe played her next word, managing "euchre" using the "r" I had just laid down. "This is what happens when you actually read as a kid," Zoe teased me.

"Hey, I read books. I just didn't read the same books you did."

"That is true. You loved *Goosebumps* more than anything in the world, whereas they scared the crap out of me."

"What did you read at Charlie's age, then?" Mom asked Zoe.

"*Babysitter's Club*," I replied immediately. "Zoe had every single one of those books. She devoured them constantly. Every time we had a spare minute, or whenever Zoe finished her work before the rest of us—which was always—she'd pull one out of her desk and be nose deep in it."

"That's true," Zoe said with a grin. "I always thought I was a Stacey. You, on the other hand, were a total Kristy."

"I don't know what those names mean, but sure, I'll agree with that."

"Kristy was the bossy one who was really good at softball, and a natural leader, but under that hard exterior was a heart of gold," Zoe said. "And that's you in a nutshell."

I leaned over and rested my head on her shoulder. "You're too nice. Also, I don't know how to play softball."

Zoe laughed while Mom played her pieces, looking kindly over at the two of us.

"How you've both grown," she said. "The two of you used to play in the yard like this, twenty years ago. It's great to see how you've turned out. Zoe, who's a doctor now, and Charlie, who's… still finding her way in life, but getting there."

"Well, that suddenly sounds pathetic when you put me up next to Zoe," I said with a laugh.

But Zoe shook her head. "It's not," she said. "Life isn't a race. It isn't as if we're running off a checklist and the goal is to tick everything off as fast as possible. Life is a journey. And if it takes you a little bit longer to get to the part of your journey where you've figured out what you want to do, then so be it."

"Well said," Mom agreed, nodding and taking another sip of wine. "Frankly, I'm glad life has taken you to a point where you've come back to the island. Your father would be proud of you, you know?"

I gulped hard, as just the mention of my father risked starting the tears flowing. "Yeah," I managed to stammer out. "Yeah, I know."

"Anyway, this isn't a night for deep topics. I've had enough of that for a few days. I want to hear all of Charlie's horror stories from working at the ice cream shop."

I laughed. "You'll be disappointed to hear I don't have all that many. I mean, apart from my customer who was murdered, but that didn't even happen in the shop. Just your run-of-the-mill story of people wanting thirty different samples, kids running wild, that sort of thing."

"Well, I'm sure you'll eventually get some crazies," Zoe said with a grin. "After all, there are bound to be some awful, awful children out there who try and steal a pint one day."

I sent Zoe a death glare, turning my head so Mom couldn't see, while she grinned at me mischievously.

"I can't believe that happens," Mom said, shaking her head. "What kind of horrible child would do something like that?"

"Leslie told me you know, Mom," I said pointedly. "She said you came in and paid for the pint of ice cream later that day."

"Oh. Well, I've been secretly guilt tripping you about that for years. I guess I can't do that anymore."

"If it makes you feel any better, I haven't actually stolen anything since that pint of ice cream. I like to pretend I'm a big badass, but I felt bad about it for months after," I admitted.

Mom laughed. "I bet. Leslie is a good woman. I'm glad her business is doing well."

I nodded. "I mean, I don't exactly know all the details of her financials, but from what I can tell, she's doing very well for herself. She has a good mix of loyal locals and foot traffic from tourists, and as soon as you taste the ice cream, you can see why. It's *delicious*. Her daughter makes most of it in the back, and it's incredible. I've never had ice cream that good in my life."

"Yes, I've stopped by for a scoop from time to time when I'm in that part of town and have never been disappointed," Mom agreed.

"I should stop by tomorrow morning," Zoe mused.

"You should. It's my day off though, so I won't be able to give you a free cone."

"Well, in that case, I'll wait a couple days," Zoe said.

"Not so much for the free cone but because I want to make you wait on me."

I laughed. "I'll take good care of you, like you did to me…" I trailed off. I still hadn't told Mom about being Tased.

"When I picked you up from the airport? Yeah," Zoe said, immediately picking up on my discomfort and covering for me.

This was why Zoe was my best friend. I could stick my foot in my mouth, and she'd gracefully remove it and make me look like a normal human being once more.

"Right," Mom said, nodding as she played another word and then took another sip of wine. "Well, all in all, I think you turned out okay, Charlie."

"Thanks, Mom," I said with a chuckle as I looked at the board. This was nice. It was really nice.

Chapter 21

The next day, since it was my day off, I slept in until almost ten. By the time I stumbled out of bed, had a shower, and started looking halfway normal, Zoe was just getting ready for her noon shift at the hospital.

Mom had gone off to have lunch with a friend, which meant I was soon to be on my own in the house.

"I hope it's still okay that I'm staying here," Zoe said. "I can leave if I'm intruding."

"Of course not," I said, waving my hand. "You stay here for as long as you need. And I'm not just offering because I know it's not my house; my mom would say the same thing. You can ask her yourself if you're not sure. But there's no way you're going back to that creepy stalker apartment, ever. Or at least, not until you're ready."

Zoe flashed me a grateful smile. "You have no idea how much I appreciate this."

"I really do. You tell me unnecessarily every single day."

"Fair point. Okay, well, I'm going to work. I'll be back later tonight."

"See you," I said as I went to the kitchen to pour myself a bowl of cereal.

When I finished eating, I noticed Coco following me around.

"Want to go for a walk?" I asked.

She immediately perked up at the sound of the magic word. Doing laps around my legs, Coco danced to and fro, announcing to me that yes, she did, in fact, want to go for a walk.

"All right, let's go then," I said, grabbing the leash and slipping on my shoes.

Coco hopped up on her hind legs in excitement, doing laps around me once more, but I eventually managed to grab a hold of her and clip the leash onto her collar. I opened the door, and she lunged for freedom, straining at the leash as I struggled to lock the door behind us while not simultaneously having my arm ripped off.

I laughed as I ran with Coco along the walkway leading to the street until I reached the sidewalk and collided directly with somebody.

"Oof," I said, stumbling into a man's body. I might have fallen to the ground, having been knocked off balance, but the man's arms grabbed me firmly around the waist and kept me upright. Then embarrassment hit me as I realized what I'd done. "I'm so sorry. Are you all right?" I asked. I looked up to find myself staring directly into Jake's laughing eyes.

"I'm fine. Are you?"

"Yeah," I replied, brushing myself off and quickly stepping away from him.

Coco, for her part, didn't seem to care at all about what had just happened and was happily sniffing the hedge at the edge of the property.

"What are you doing here?"

"Looking for you, actually."

"Oh?" I said, my eyebrows rising. "What happened? Did you and your partner run out of innocent people to Taser?"

"Ha ha, you're hilarious," Jake replied. "Seriously though, I was at the station this morning, and I saw Josh Newman had been arrested. Is Zoe all right?"

I nodded. "Yeah, no thanks to the cops. Newman broke into her apartment while we were picking up some stuff and tried to attack her. We were able to take him down."

"I'm glad you're both okay," Jake said. "You're going to have to testify at his trial. You know that, right?"

"Yeah, it's great. Zoe's a victim of a crime, and she's going to get to continue reliving the experience for months or even years," I replied.

"The system isn't perfect," Jake conceded. "I know that as well as anyone."

"Good. Because Zoe did everything she was supposed to. She got the restraining order. When he broke the rules, she called the cops. And they did nothing. And he broke into her place to try and attack her. You're all the same, cops. You get involved after the fact. And meanwhile, in all of this, *I'm* the only person in this story who's actually been attacked by a cop. Not the guy who stalked my friend for days and was finally arrested inside her apartment. Me."

"The person who was trespassing on a crime scene, looking for clues," Jake pointed out.

"I certainly didn't see anything saying we weren't allowed to be there."

"You were investigating a murder that you are not supposed to be involved in."

"I didn't realize that was illegal or that it gave your partner the right to use a weapon against me."

I stared Jake down, neither one of us willing to back down.

"Look," he finally said. "I am sorry for what happened to you at the park, and I am sorry about what happened with Zoe. But the important thing is that Josh Newman is behind bars and likely will be for a long time."

"Yeah, thanks to a baseball bat in Zoe's apartment," I replied. "I don't know why you came here, but if it was to get kudos for what the police department did, you're way off the mark."

"I came here to make sure you're both fine, all right? I know things didn't go the way you'd hoped. Hell, they didn't go the way I hoped, either. But I can't just go around breaking the rules and regulations of the police department. We have rules in place, and they have to be obeyed."

"Right. It's too bad those rules don't seem to protect victims until after it's too late."

"Is the system perfect? No. But it's the best one we've got."

"Is that where it ends, then? Well, it's good enough, so let's not strive for better?"

"That's not what I said," Jake snapped. "Of course we need to strive for better. But right now, at this moment, this is what we've got, and I can't go play cowboy like you are, trying to solve this murder case, because the difference between us is I'd get fired for doing some of the things you do."

I huffed, shaking my head. "Fine. But don't come here looking for accolades because Josh is in jail. He should have been in jail earlier, and my best friend shouldn't be staying here because she's too scared to go back into her apartment."

"I'm not here looking for accolades," Jake replied. "I just came to check on you. Not for praise."

Okay, if I thought about it, I had to admit that he had a point. He had only actually asked after Zoe and me to make sure we were all right. So why was I so upset at seeing him? Was it because of the way my heart skipped a bit when I saw him or the way my stomach had done a flip when I realized his were the arms holding me upright?

No. I pushed those thoughts out of my head. I'd just woken up on the wrong side of the bed. That had to be it.

"Fine," I replied. "We're both okay. Newman is in jail, and I just hope that one day, Zoe can convince herself to get back into that apartment. Or maybe she won't. But either way, it's messed with her life. It's messed with her mind. And she's too nice a person to deserve that."

"She is," Jake agreed. "No one deserves that."

I nodded. "How's your investigation into the murder going?"

Jake looked at me curiously. "Seriously? You really have no shame. First of all, I can't tell you. Secondly, I wouldn't tell you anything even if I could."

"Hey, I'm not saying I'm still investigating," I said, holding up my hands. Of course, I wasn't saying I *wasn't* investigating, either.

"Good. Because this is a murder case, and I don't want you looking for trouble. Trouble seems to find you anyway. You don't need to go hunting for it."

"And what's that supposed to mean?" I asked, placing my hands on my hips.

"Since I've known you, you've trespassed on a crime scene, been Tasered, and were involved in taking down a criminal stalking your friend, and that's only the stuff I know about. I'm sure there's more."

"I moved to Maui because gangsters in Seattle were trying to kill me and sent me a finger in the mail," I added. "You forgot that part. But don't tell anyone else that part; I wouldn't be surprised if the gangsters are still after me and just don't know where I went."

Jake gave me a long, hard look as if he was either trying to figure out whether I was telling the truth or trying to process what I'd just told him.

"You're the one," he said after a minute. "I heard about that. You shot the guy's brother when he was trying to rob a jewelry store."

"That's me: Miss Customer Service," I deadpanned. "When I found the finger on my doorstep, I bailed. I like all my appendages, and the rest of me. I'd like them all to stay attached."

"And so you turned into my problem."

"Excuse me, but I don't see how anything I've done so far makes me a *problem*. If anyone here is the problem, it's your partner."

Jake laughed. "Fine. Bad choice of words. But trouble seems to find you wherever you go."

"Trouble finding me does not make me trouble."

"Maybe, but where there's smoke, there's fire."

I crossed my arms. "Or maybe it's just smoke caused by someone else's fire."

"Maybe," Jake said with a laugh. "Anyway, on a more serious note, it's good you left Seattle. No matter how much trouble you might wind up finding yourself in here, it's unlikely to be as bad as what was waiting for you over there."

I nodded. "The woman assigned the case tried to get me to stay, although she didn't try very hard. She promised me the police would protect me, but there was no way. There's a difference between protection and prosecution after a crime is committed. And in my experience, the police have a long way to go when it comes to the former."

"You're not wrong," Jake agreed, and the two of us began walking in step together in the direction of the beach. "However, at the same time, our hands are tied by the system somewhat. We can't go around arresting people because they *might* commit a crime in the future. That's some real *Minority Report* stuff, and it goes against most of the principles of this country."

"True," I conceded. "I'm not sure there is a simple answer. But the system as it stands is far from perfect."

"You won't find any argument here," Jake replied. "And if there's a way to make it better, I'll do my best to make it happen. But unfortunately, that's usually above my pay grade."

"Like the councilmembers," I said.

Jake gave me a disapproving stare.

"I was at their meeting yesterday. I figured I might as well involve myself in local politics if I'm going to be staying here a while."

"Right. I really believe civic-mindedness was your primary motivation," Jake replied, his tone making it obvious he didn't believe me in the least.

"Well, at least I wasn't the one taken away by the cops after threatening some of the councilmembers," I said.

Jake nodded. "No kidding. I heard it was quite the kerfuffle."

"Who was assigned to the search for the bribery money?" I asked as we reached the beach.

Coco started pulling to go play in the sand—there were always a million things for her to sniff on the beach —and Jake followed me.

"An independent investigator was assigned," he replied. "Someone from Oahu who had never had any dealings with anyone involved."

"Think he could have been paid off to overlook something?" I asked.

Jake shook his head. "No. We had to look into him for our investigation. He seems clean. Besides, who would have paid him off? MacMahon didn't care; he got his approval. No matter what happened after that vote, he could build his stupid hotel."

"I don't know," I said slowly. "People here *really* hate the idea of it. I think if it came out that the councilmembers had been bribed, there would have been too much pressure from residents to reverse the decision."

"That's possible," Jake admitted. "I'm not completely up to date on the nuances of civic law here in Maui County."

I laughed. "Well, I was at that meeting last night, and trust me, there was almost a mutiny right then and there. People aren't happy about MacMahon having gotten the right to build that resort, and they shouldn't be. The councilmembers who voted for it were bribed."

Jake gave me a hard look. "Do you know that for sure, or are you just speculating?"

"Well, I overheard Natalie Lee and Janice Evers talking about it in the bathroom last night. They received a payoff, one hundred percent."

Jake let out a low whistle. "I'm guessing you don't have any proof of this? Did they say anything about where the money might be? This is big news."

I shook my head. "They mentioned an overseas account, but that's it. I was hiding in a stall and wasn't exactly going to pop my head out and ask them to be more explicit in their admission to receiving the proceeds of a crime."

"I guess that makes sense. Well, it's good to know that the bribery happened. I'm going to report it to my superior, though I'm not sure there's all that much we can do. Especially since the independent investigator didn't find anything. We have police auditors on staff, but I doubt they'd find anything if the specialist brought in from Oahu didn't."

"Yeah," I said. "Unfortunately, unless one of them killed him, I don't think you're ever going to find the proof you need to arrest them."

"It's too bad," Jake said. "I agree that the project shouldn't happen. It would be a detriment to the town, a detriment to the whole island. We need tourists, and we need these hotels, but we don't need them in Kihei. Tourism has to balance with the needs of the local community, and this project upsets that balance."

"Do you think that was the motivation behind MacMahon's murder?" I asked.

Jake gave me a knowing look. "You do realize I already told you I can't talk about an open investigation, don't you?"

"Sure, but I figured maybe I'd catch you off guard," I admitted with a shrug.

Jake laughed good-naturedly. "You're something else. You know that, right?"

"I'm going to take it as a compliment."

"It was meant as one."

The words were so unexpected coming from Jake that I opened and closed my mouth a couple of times, trying to come up with a reply as a blush crawled up the back of my neck. I *really* hoped he didn't spot it.

Instead, I chose that exact moment to trip on nothing at all, and I fell face-first into the sand.

I lay there for a second instead of getting up, allowing the lack of dignity to *really* sink in.

Coco, immediately spotting that for once I was at ground level like she was, took advantage of the fact by jumping onto my back just to truly let it sink in how low I'd fallen.

"Are you okay?" Jake asked.

I propped myself up onto my arms so as to avoid getting a mouthful of sand when I answered. "I'm good, thanks."

He helped me up, with Coco jumping excitedly around me as if it was the best thing that had ever happened to her. I found a stick on the ground a few feet away that I threw for her. Coco chased excitedly after it while I set about slapping at my clothes, trying to get the sand to fall back down onto the beach. I looked up at Jake, who was obviously biting back a laugh.

"Go ahead," I said, moving my hands in a circular motion while rolling my eyes. "You can laugh. I won't be insulted."

"No, no," he insisted, biting a corner of his lip while the other end tilted upward into a smile. "I'm not laughing at you. It wasn't that funny. I swear."

"I can tell you're lying."

"I am lying—that was hilarious—but I'm only trying to make you feel better."

Okay, I had to look on the bright side. I'd tripped and fallen face-first onto the beach, but at least we'd moved past the compliment comment without it being awkward.

"It's fine. Don't worry. I'm fine. Just a slightly bruised

ego."

"I won't tell anyone this happened if you don't," Jake said with a laugh. "Anyway, I have to get going. I'm meeting Liam down at the station."

"Got another hard day of Tasering innocent people in front of him, has he?" I asked.

Jake sighed. "Look, I know that situation sucked, but… you have to get over it."

"I have to get over a potentially lethal weapon discharging thousands of volts of electricity into my body? No, I don't. Especially when it was aimed at a lady in her seventies. Your partner wanted to play Zeus, and that's okay, but you have to understand that Zeus was a dick. An enormous, giant dick, and no one likes him."

"All right, all right. You've got a point. Although I don't think Liam really has as much power as Zeus, luckily."

"There are a whole lot of reasons why Zeus was super problematic."

"You're not wrong. Anyway, I'll see you around. If you or Zoe need anything, call me whenever. I know Josh is in prison, and hopefully things will stay that way. I'll keep you informed of what happens."

"Thanks."

Jake gave me a quick wave as he half jogged back toward the street. I watched as he left. I couldn't quite figure him out.

Well, so long as he stayed out of the way while I found James MacMahon's killer, that was fine. And so long as his partner Liam stayed far, far away as well.

Chapter 22

I continued walking down the beach with Coco until we eventually reached the park where James MacMahon had been stabbed and where I'd been Tased a few days later.

I clenched my fists in anger as I looked out to where it had happened but quickly moved on. Whatever. There wasn't a chance in hell that I'd ever forgive him for it, but right now, I had to focus on James MacMahon's death.

I ran through everything I knew about the man as I stared at the spot where he had been killed. He had come into the ice cream store desperate for a cab because someone had hacked his Uber account. He couldn't get into it. Okay, fine. He was on the phone with Alice, and she was booking him another flight that would be ready when he got to the airport.

Suddenly, I thought of something.

"Oh, Coco," I said, looking at my dog. "I think we need to drop you right off home."

Coco looked up at me happily, her tongue hanging out of her mouth, lined with sand.

I took off in the other direction, running back toward Mom's place, with Coco following me, her little legs moving as fast as they could carry her. I imagined myself in a movie right now, speeding toward the climax, but the reality was a bit different. I managed to get about two hundred yards before I had to stop and rest, panting as I placed my hands on my knees and gasped, trying to get more air into my lungs. I really needed to exercise more. Or at all.

Making it the rest of the way home at a quick walking pace—it wouldn't have looked quite as good in a movie, but at least I didn't risk keeling over and dying from a heart attack—I dropped off Coco and texted Rosie to meet me at Dot's place. It was an emergency.

Mom had taken the car, so I walked over to Dot's as fast as I could.

"Who is this, Darth Vader?" Dot asked when I rang up to her apartment.

"I'll use the Force against you if you don't let me in," I replied.

"Come on up."

Rosie must have been waiting for me, because as soon as I reached the front door, she opened it for me. Her expression was all business.

"What is it?"

"Dot, you looked up flight manifests somehow, right?"

"Yes," Dot replied.

"Are you able to see who had a ticket for a flight or who was *on* a flight?"

"Both."

"I need you to check something for me: all flights between the islands and New York City the night James MacMahon was killed."

"It'll take a little bit, but sure. Get comfortable."

She sat down at her work station and turned on all four monitors. I had no idea what she was doing, but her fingers flew over the keyboard.

"Did you run here?" Rosie asked me, pouring me a glass of water and handing it over while Dot worked.

"Yeah, I totally did," I lied, leaning my head back slightly as I downed the entire glass in one gulp.

"What have you thought of?" Rosie said. "You have to have an idea."

"I do," I replied, nodding. And with that, I outlined everything I had figured out to Rosie.

She nodded slowly. "You might be onto something there," she said.

"If you are, we have to move quickly," Dot said. "There isn't much time."

"That's why I said it was an emergency," I said with a grin.

Sure enough, half an hour later, we had our answer.

"I've looked at the purchase logs for every single flight off this archipelago that night," Dot said. "Just to be safe. No James MacMahon on any of them."

"The police would already know this," I said slowly. "So that means they haven't figured out who it is."

"We can't go to the police. We have to get proof ourselves," Rosie said.

"Right," Dot replied. "After all, we've got to collect that reward. Let's go get some proof."

"Hold up. Are you sure you both want to come along?" I asked. "After all, this part is probably pretty dangerous."

"And why would that stop us?" Dot asked, a hand on her hip.

"Well, I dunno. You're kind of… you know…"

"Old?" Dot asked, her eyebrows rising.

"You're the one who said it, not me."

"Honey, old and cowardly aren't the same thing," Dot replied. "Of course we're coming. Heck, I haven't had this much of an adventure since 1977, when Don Carols went to Oahu and stole… you know what, maybe that's a story for another day."

"Uh, what? That sounds like a story that totally needs to be told today," I said.

But Dot shook her head. "Forget I said anything. Maybe another time."

If it hadn't been for the fact that we were about to confront a killer, I probably would have pressed the point more. I was always up for a good story. But there were more important things on my mind, and we were so close to the hundred grand I could practically taste it.

The three of us got into Rosie's car, and she began driving. "We need Alice to confess to her crime, and we need to record it. That's the best proof we can get."

Alice Doherty was our killer. I was sure of it. Now I just had to prove it.

WE REACHED THE LOBBY OF THE HOTEL WHERE SHE was staying, and Rosie motioned for me to follow and for Dot to stay back. We went straight to the front desk, where Rosie took over.

"Hello, dear," she told the woman working, making her voice sound a tad more old and croaky than usual. "I'm here to visit my granddaughter with my caregiver, but she said she might be leaving soon. Could you let me know if she's still here? Room 522."

The woman at the front desk smiled kindly on Rosie. "Of course, ma'am. Let me check for you."

"Thank you, dear. It's been so long since I've seen Alice, and what with everything that's gone on, I'm sure she'd love to see a familiar face."

"I imagine so," the woman said with a kind smile. "She's due to check out tomorrow morning, so you're welcome to go right on up to see her."

"Thank you for the help," Rosie croaked, turning around slowly and grabbing my arm, pretending to need it for support.

I smiled at the woman as well as I led Rosie toward the elevators. Dot followed after us, pretending she didn't know us.

When the three of us were finally headed up to the fifth floor to see Alice, we dropped the act. "She's leaving tomorrow," Rosie told Dot.

"That means we need to get the confession out of her today."

The three of us were walking down the hall when I

heard the click of a door closing and spotted a familiar face headed toward us. It was Alice. She didn't look especially pleased to see us.

"Hi," she said. "I was just heading down for lunch."

"Would you mind if we joined you?" Rosie said. "We won't be long. We just had a few more questions to ask about James."

Alice sighed, obviously not wanting to eat with us. I suspected she was trying to get us to withdraw our invitation, but when we didn't, she relented.

"I guess that's fine," she finally said. "I was really hoping to enjoy my last lunch here at the hotel."

"Well, we won't stop you," Rosie said. "We'll be quick."

"I just forgot something real quick," Alice said. "One moment."

She went back into her room, I suspected hoping that the three of us would lose interest and leave, but when she came back a few minutes later, we were still waiting for her in the hall.

"So you're heading back to New York tomorrow?" Dot asked.

Alice nodded. "Yes. I'm quite relieved. I can't wait to sleep in my own bed and put this all behind me."

The four of us rode the elevator down and headed to the restaurant, where Alice had a reservation.

"I'm afraid I have three people accompanying me. Is that all right?" Alice asked the hostess, obviously hoping we'd be told to eat elsewhere.

"That's fine," the hostess replied. "We can easily

change your seating arrangements to accommodate your guests."

Alice thanked the waitress, but I couldn't help but notice her lips were pressed into a thin line. The last time she had seen us, she had pretended to be friendly and happy to help. This time, she was much less so. I couldn't exactly blame her; she was very close to getting off the island and getting away with the murder she had committed. Having to speak to us and pretend that she was innocent was not in her plans.

We were led to a table shaded by an umbrella as the waves beat against the coast nearby. My stomach grumbled, and I realized I was hungry, but I was still completely unable to focus on the menu.

The waitress came by with a pitcher of water a few minutes later, and I ordered some sort of pasta—I really didn't pay much attention to what—and focused on Alice, who ordered a bottle of red wine for the table.

Now that we were outside and settled, she seemed a little bit more comfortable. Still, she sat fumbling with her purse, but now she smiled as the waitress came by with the bottle of wine.

"Sorry if I was a little brusque before," she said. "It's just… I'm really looking forward to being back home and not having to talk about James and what happened to him anymore. There are still times when I can't believe it happened, you know? Hence the wine. It's early in the day, I know, but I figured I could use a drink. And of course, this is my apology."

"Of course," Rosie murmured soothingly, like a kindly grandmother. "No apology needed. We completely understand. And we don't want you to have to relive anything you're not comfortable with."

"Thanks," Alice said. "I have to say, of everyone who's come around asking questions, you've been the nicest by far."

"There have been others who found you?" I asked.

Alice nodded. "Yes. Not a lot, but a few. One especially, a private investigator, was incredibly rude. She kept threatening to arrest me if I didn't answer her questions."

"I think I met her the other day," I said wryly. "Black, curly hair, kind of looked like a white version of the Hulk?"

"That was her," Alice confirmed, nodding. "It was unbelievable, really, the things she asked me. She kept accusing me of not telling her everything I knew and that she knew I was in the taxi with James and that I'd run away after he was stabbed."

I laughed. "Well, that's ridiculous." I had seen James get into the taxi and drive off. Besides, Alice had to have texted James to meet her at the park.

"It's completely insane. But this woman was crazy. I honestly thought she was going to have the cops called on me. I didn't go back out onto the beach by myself after that." Alice wrapped her arms around herself. "It's part of why I'm happy to go home."

"I can imagine," I said.

The waitress came by with our food. She placed it in front of us, and I started eating, pouring myself a glass of water as well. After all, if we were about to make a hundred grand, I could actually afford a meal or two at a restaurant like this.

The four of us ate in comfortable silence for a little while, until eventually, our plates about half-eaten, Alice leaned back in her chair. "So, what did you want to ask me about?"

Dot had assured me that she was going to get the recording—Hawaii being a one-party state, we didn't have to disclose to Alice that we were recording her. We only needed to get her confession. And I was going to do it.

"James MacMahon assaulted you, didn't he?" I asked her quietly. "He tried to force himself on you."

Alice's back immediately stiffened. "Why would you suggest something like that?" she hissed.

"It was something I heard, a comment in passing that made me realize that all men like him go for their secretaries at some point. And here you are, in Hawaii with your boss. In the same hotel. He can't have let that go."

"You're wrong," Alice said, but her face betrayed that she was lying. She couldn't believe I'd figured it out.

"I don't think I am."

"Well, that's too bad. You are wrong. James never did anything of the sort. He was always a gentleman."

"Please. He's been in trouble for that sort of thing before. I did my research. A woman sued him when he tried to force himself on her at a conference."

Alice still refused to budge. "That woman was a liar looking to make headlines. He never did anything to me."

"He did, though. And you couldn't stand it. That day at the restaurant, you'd had enough. You took the knife with the mother-of-pearl handle, you slipped it into your purse, and later that afternoon, you stabbed him. I know you didn't actually book him a flight off the island. That was your biggest mistake. You should have booked a flight, any flight. But you never did, because you knew he was never getting off… off…"

I trailed off, suddenly having a mental blank. Where were we? In fact, everything seemed hazy. I was having more and more trouble concentrating, and I looked up at Alice, confused. She gave me the creepiest smile I have ever seen.

Chapter 23

"Your biggest mistake was thinking you would get me to confess," she said. She looked around carefully to make sure we weren't being watched, then flashed a gun at the three of us. "Now, we're all going to leave here, nice and easy, and anyone who doesn't pretend that everything is hunky dory is dead. Got it?"

I looked around at my companions. I couldn't really remember their names. One of them was Comma? No, that wasn't right. They both looked a bit out of it, like me, and I realized we'd been drugged.

Uh oh.

"I said, do you understand?"

I nodded. I might have some sort of drug in my system, and I couldn't really think, but "gun" was still pretty understandable, no matter how much brain fog I had. Alice had a gun, and there was nothing I could do about it.

"Come on," she ordered. "Everyone up, and leave like there's nothing wrong."

I stood up, and my legs felt like lead. I was vaguely aware of the other two ladies standing next to me, and we followed after Alice, who stopped to sign for our meal on her room tab.

"Thanks for coming, I hope you enjoyed your meal," the waitress said with a smile.

"Thanks," I heard myself reply. "You too."

We were almost out of the hotel before I realized that was totally not an appropriate response. Oh well, it was too late to do anything about it now.

Alice led us to a huge SUV in the parking lot. She opened the back and motioned for us to get in. There was space for all three of us and a row of seats between us and the driver's seat.

"If I see any of you try and get close to me, you die," Alice said, shutting the door on us.

She pulled away from the lot and began driving while I tried to get my brain to work. My whole body felt like lead. It was like I'd just woken up with the world's worst hangover, and I doubted Alice was going to stop off at McDonald's to grab a greasy breakfast to make me feel better.

Alice was the killer. And she was taking us somewhere. I didn't know where we were headed, but I had a feeling it wasn't good.

Even in my current state, I knew that.

Eventually, the low hum of the concrete beneath us turned into more of a rattling; we had moved from concrete onto a dirt road. This didn't bode well for my chances of survival. If I wanted to get out of this alive, I was going to have to do something. I just didn't have the energy for it. My stomach began to grumble as nausea built up inside of me. I pushed it aside.

That was when I realized Alice was talking. She was saying something from her spot in the front of the SUV.

"You were right, you know. He did try to rape me. I managed to fight him off, but that was the last straw, you know? I'd had it. I knew he had done it to other women. I was his secretary. I was the one who passed things to his lawyer—the one he personally kept on retainer, not the ones that the firm had on hand. I was the one who saw the paperwork as it came through, the NDAs. He paid those women millions to keep their mouths shut. And when he did it to me, you know what he said?"

Alice waited for a moment, as if expecting any of us to answer, and then gave a high, piercing laugh with no humor in it. "He told me to get lost. He told me that unlike those other women, I was his secretary. He said society practically expected us to be banging and that he would portray me as the jealous love who had consented to sex but was mad when she found out about his other affairs. He said he wasn't going to pay me off when he didn't even get the goods. Can you believe it? James MacMahon was a piece of crap. So when we came to Hawaii, I knew this was my chance."

Alice paused for a moment, taking a tight corner. Some sort of switchback.

A moment later, she continued. "I'd had it. I'd had it with him. Everyone thought he was great. He was so charismatic. Sure, in front of other people. In private, he was a dick. So when, on top of everything else, he told me he wasn't going to pay me *and* would ruin my life if I went to the papers, I decided I was going to kill him. We came here, and to my dismay, the trip was practically over before it began. As it turned out, everyone on this island hated James. He couldn't charisma his way out of that much hatred. He had bribed three members of the city council to get the votes to approve his hotel, but that didn't turn public opinion in favor of the development. So he wanted to go home early. I told him all the flights were booked. Then, I changed the password on his Uber account. I wanted him as flustered as possible so that he wouldn't be thinking straight. I told him to meet me at the park, that I couldn't get my email account to work and that I could meet him with the printed documents. And then I stabbed him."

Alice laughed again, that same psychotic laugh. "The look on his face. It was glorious. He couldn't believe it was me. He knew he was dying. I saw him rasp his last breath, and as soon as he collapsed, I ran. No one believed it was me. No one ever looks at the secretary. The first time you three came by, you were all so sympathetic. You couldn't have thought it was me. I was so innocent. And then the second time, I knew you were onto me. And I just can't have that. But that's okay. At least now you know the truth. It's too bad you're not going to live to tell anyone about it."

Well, that was the confirmation I didn't exactly need. Alice had no intention of letting us leave here alive. I was going to die here, on Maui. The island that had taken my father was going to take me too. I should have stayed in Seattle. Who knew that gangsters were probably less dangerous than this psycho?

Alice began slowing down. My best chance for survival would be to attack as soon as she opened the back of the SUV. I had to do whatever I could to bring her down. I mean, what did I have to lose? If she shot me immediately, the death might be quicker than whatever she had planned.

I did my best to psych myself up. As soon as that back door opened, I had to be ready to pounce. A moment later, the rear door started moving upward. Alice was behind it. I jumped out of the car as fast as I could, but instead of rushing forward and tackling Alice, I spewed vomit all over her.

"What the hell?" she shouted, spreading her arms as she looked down at her front in disgust. "What is *wrong* with you?"

Well, it wasn't exactly the way I'd planned to get her guard down, but whatever worked was fine with me. I was nauseous, and my brain was still foggy as anything. I wanted to lie down in the dirt and have a nap. But I didn't have the chance. I rushed forward and shoved Alice as hard as I could. She stumbled.

Out of the corner of my eye, I spotted one of the older women I was with. Rose? Rosetta Stone? No. Something like that. She moved like a fox, darting behind Alice. Then, she put one hand on either side of her neck and twisted.

Just like that, the light in Alice's eyes disappeared. Her mouth was shaped in an "O" of surprise, and her neck hung at a strange, unnatural angle.

The woman dropped the body to the ground, and I

stared at it, not entirely realizing what I was looking at just yet.

"Right," the woman said. "Charlie, Dot, we'd best be getting the two of you to a hospital."

And that was when everything went black.

Chapter 24

For the second time in a week, I woke up to the rhythmic beeping of a heart rate monitor.

I kept my eyes closed for a second. It was like a fraternity had decided to have a house party inside my head. I took a couple deep breaths then heard Mom's voice.

"Charlotte? Are you waking up?"

I groaned and fluttered my eyelids open. They landed on Mom's face, lined with worry.

"Oh, Charlie. Oh, I'm so glad you're awake."

Mom simultaneously looked like she wanted to lean over and hug me but realized I was so fragile I might snap in half if she tried. She moved back and forth in her chair and eventually decided it was worth the risk. She reached over and smothered me with her body, holding me close to her.

I hugged her back, closing my eyes as I breathed in the scent of her hair.

"What happened?" I asked Mom.

She shook her head. "Not now, honey. Just know that you're safe. Zoe is taking good care of you. She's been stopping by every fifteen minutes to see if you're awake yet. She should be by soon."

"Where are Dot and Rosie?" I mumbled.

"Dorothy is in the bed next to you," Mom said quietly. "She didn't handle the drug as well as you did, and she's still out of it. The doctors think she'll be fine."

"And Rosie?"

"She's just gone out to get some food."

"What happened to Alice?"

"The woman who tried to kill you? She's dead."

It all came flooding back. It was Rosie who had snuck up behind Alice. She had snapped her neck like a twig. Who *was* Rosie?

I leaned back in the hospital bed and sighed.

"That's right, honey. Get some rest. I'll be here with you."

And with that, I passed out again.

When I woke up once more, Mom was still in her seat, listening to an audiobook. As soon as she saw I'd opened my eyes, she yanked the headphones from her ears. "How are you feeling, honey?"

"I'm okay, thanks," I said. "You can go home. I'll be okay. You must be exhausted."

Mom's eyes were red, with black bags sagging beneath them. She looked like she'd aged a decade in the last twenty-four hours. Still, she smiled, creases lining the corner of her mouth. "I'm all right."

"I'm serious, Mom. I'm fine. Go home and get some sleep."

"Are you sure, dear?"

I nodded. "I'll probably be released soon anyway."

"Well, you give me a call if you need a ride, okay? I love you, honey. I'm glad you're okay."

"I love you too, Mom," I whispered.

As soon as my mom left the room, Rosie entered. She sat in the seat that had just been occupied by my mother. "How are you feeling?"

"Well, it's not as bad as when I got Tasered," I replied with a small smile.

Rosie laughed lightly. "It's nice to see the Rohypnol didn't dull your sense of humor."

"Rohypnol? Alice gave us a date-rape drug?"

Rosie nodded. "She must have slipped it into the wine when the waitress was handing out the food."

I leaned back in the bed and groaned. "Great. Is Dot okay?"

"She should be," Rosie said, her expression turning grim. "It was worse for her, though. She was more badly affected by the drug. But the doctors aren't worried."

"I'm glad she's going to be okay," I said.

"Me too."

I looked at Rosie. "How come you weren't affected by it at all? You…" My voice trailed off. I wasn't really sure how to phrase the next part of it. "You ran behind her and snapped her neck like it was nothing." How do you ask someone about that?

Rosie gave me a small smile. "I only pretended to drink the wine."

"Of course. That makes sense. But still. There's something you're not telling me."

"There's a lot I haven't told you," Rosie said, leaning back in the chair with a sigh. "And I suppose you deserve to know. After all, you're a smart cookie. You're the one who figured out Alice was the killer. That was great work."

"Thanks," I said, waiting.

Rosie's eyes settled on a spot on the far wall, but she obviously wasn't seeing anything. She was in the past. "My real name isn't Rosemary Williams."

"I kind of figured that," I said with a wry smile. "What are you, some kind of retired CIA agent?"

Rosie laughed. "Oh, dear me, no. I was KGB." The stunned expression on my face couldn't have been subtle, because Rosie grinned and said, "*That* you weren't expecting, were you?"

"KGB? As in the Russians?"

"Soviet, yes. I was born in Stalingrad, which is now called St. Petersburg. As a child, I exceled in mathematics and languages. I was recruited into a program and trained as a teenager to live in America. I was supposed to infiltrate the country and spy on the government by working inside of it."

"Holy crap, that actually happened? That wasn't just the plotline for *The Americans*?"

"No, it was very much a real thing. And I was dedicated to my work. I was assigned to Honolulu, where I was to try and get a job working at the Navy base at Pearl Harbor. And I managed it. However, there was one thing the Russians did not count on."

"And what was that?"

"That I would fall in love with the country I was

assigned to betray. Do you know what it was like, living in St. Petersburg?"

"I can't imagine it looked like this."

Rosie gave me a wry smile. "No, it did not. During the war, my brother died in the harsh winter of forty-two. My aunt and uncle and both their children died during the Siege of Leningrad. My cousins, Misha and Sergei. It was a harsh life. And here, in Hawaii, the opposite. Life was simple. People were happy. Coca-Cola was like a happy explosion of joy with every sip. I had never had a milkshake before. And the people, they were simply so free. Everyone had the opportunity to do whatever they wanted. I wanted that life for myself. And I wanted it permanently."

"So what did you do?"

"I defected," Rosie replied with a shrug. "Of course, it was not official. No one from the government knows where I came from, and my identity is so airtight they would never be able to prove it. No one from the Russian government knows where I am. I simply disappeared one day. I took on a new identity with the help of a friend that I trusted implicitly, and I moved to Maui to make it more difficult to find me. And then I began my new life."

I gaped at Rosie. How was I even supposed to respond to a story like that? "So you've just been living life like a normal American all this time?"

"I have. And it's been *wonderful*. I mean sure, I miss some aspects of my old life. There was nothing quite like the adrenaline rush that came with danger. When I stood in the line at customs at JFK—they flew me in from Western Europe to make things seem less suspicious—I thought I was going to pass out from the nerves. It was like nothing else. But ultimately, I preferred the life I lived to the one I was supposed to live."

"Wow. I mean, your KGB training came in handy."

Rosie nodded. "Yes. Alice is the first person I've killed in the United States. I didn't even think. I just acted."

"I'm glad you did," I replied. "We'd be dead otherwise."

"Obviously, you can't tell anyone else about this."

"You don't have to worry about that. Does Dot know?"

Rosie nodded. "I told her about ten years ago."

"Thanks for sharing your secret with me. Is there anything you want me to tell the cops when they come around?"

Rosie smiled. "Just pretend I never told you about my origins. From there, tell them the truth. It'll be fine."

"Are you sure?"

Rosie nodded. "Of course. Trust me. I've been in trickier situations than this before. Now, do you need anything?"

"I wouldn't say no to a burger. I'm starving. What time is it, anyway?"

"Nearly six in the morning. Your mother stayed up all night to watch you."

"She's pretty great. She can be frustrating, but overall, I'm lucky to have a mom like her."

"You certainly are. Now, I don't think I can get you a

burger. I'm not supposed to bring in any food. But then, the staff give you some leeway when you get to my age, so thanks to my big purse, I should be okay."

"Pancakes would be great if you can't get a burger."

"You can't just want an Egg McMuffin like a normal person?"

I shook my head. "Sorry. I don't like English muffins."

"Weirdo," Rosie muttered, standing up. "All right, I'll be back with some food for you in a little bit. But I don't promise pancakes. It has to be something that'll fit in my purse."

"Anything that's not hospital food is fine," I replied with a laugh. "Thanks. I appreciate it."

Rosie left, and about five minutes later, Zoe entered. "Oh, good, you're awake," she said, relief written all over her face.

"I am. Who knew that my first date-rape drug experience would have been caused by a woman?"

Zoe laughed despite herself. "You're insane. I'm glad you're okay. How are you feeling?" She instinctively looked over at the monitor displaying my vital signs.

"Good. My head still hurts a little."

"I'll have a nurse give you some stronger drugs. You're going to be fine though; now it's all about just waiting for the Rohypnol to get out of your system. The police are going to come by later to chat to you, too."

"I figured. It'll probably be Jake, since James MacMahon's murder was his case."

"I can't believe his assistant did it and that she tried to kill you," Zoe said, shaking her head. "I mean, okay, the second part I can totally believe. I told you not to go hunting murderers. I *knew* whoever did it would try to kill you."

"It's not my fault," I argued. "I'm the victim here. She gave me a date-rape drug."

Zoe raised her eyebrows. "You're the one who drank wine served to you by a murderer. Seriously, it's like you have no common sense at all. Haven't you listened to enough murder podcasts to know better?"

I opened my mouth to serve up a clever retort then closed it. Zoe had a point. I probably shouldn't have drunk the wine.

"It was an expensive bottle. I couldn't pass that up," I muttered.

Zoe rolled her eyes. "Well, I'm glad you're still here... for now. You seriously need to make better life decisions."

"This decision is going to net me a hundred grand," I pointed out. "Besides, Rosie saved my life. With my help. If I hadn't puked all over Alice when I got out of the SUV, she wouldn't have been surprised, and Rosie wouldn't have been able to sneak around without her noticing."

Zoe shook her head. "You're ridiculous. But I'm glad you're okay. I really am."

"Me too. When does your shift end?"

"Eight hours ago. But I pulled a double; I wasn't about to leave here without knowing you're fine." She reached over and squeezed my hand.

It was at that moment that I realized I had something on Maui that I didn't have anywhere else: family. I had Mom, who had stayed up all night watching me get over the effects of the drug I'd been slipped. I had Zoe, who pulled a double shift to make sure I was okay. I had Rosie, an ex-Soviet agent who was going to sneak food into a hospital for me. And I had Dot, who was in the room next door getting over the drug as well.

There was nowhere else in the world where I had this level of support. And the knowledge that these people would be with me no matter what was overwhelming. Tears welled in my eyes, and I blinked them back.

"I love you, Zoe."

"I love you too, Charlie," my best friend replied.

Maybe coming back to Maui hadn't been such a bad idea after all.

"But for the love of God, *please* stop getting yourself almost murdered."

I couldn't help myself; I burst out laughing.

Chapter 25

Rosie came back with my food about twenty minutes later.

"You know you're not supposed to have non-hospital food in here," Zoe said, giving me her best disapproving-mother look.

"Well, the hospital food sucks."

"It might suck, but it ensures that we know what's going into your body."

"Okay, Zoe, you're the best, but you're not Dr. House trying to solve a medical mystery here. I was drugged with Rohypnol, and I just need to get over it. And like with a hangover, this greasy breakfast will help me do it, and I promise it's not going to make me worse."

"Rohypnol is not like a hangover, and the food isn't going to make you better, but it's also not going to make you feel worse. So I will overlook it. *This time*."

"I don't intend to ever find myself in this hospital again," I replied. "So I agree to your terms."

"Hm, I feel like you said something similar the last time you were here. When was that? Oh yeah, like a week ago."

Rosie reached into her purse and pulled out a big bag of McDonald's. I inhaled the beautiful scent of pancakes and hash browns and smiled at her gratefully.

Zoe rolled her eyes. "Fine. You can eat it, and I'll make sure the nurses don't come in here for fifteen minutes or so."

"You're the best, Zoe."

"I know," she replied. "I'll be back soon. You should be ready for discharge in a few hours."

Zoe left, and I downed half a hash brown in a single bite.

"I'm going to check on Dot," Rosie said.

"If she wakes up, give her my best," I said.

Rosie nodded. "I will. She'll be sad that she missed you puking all over Alice."

I grinned. "You're welcome."

I was just finishing off the last of the hotcakes when Jake came in, followed by Liam.

"Sorry," I said. "I don't talk to cops who try to Taser old ladies and who successfully Taser me."

"Seriously?" Jake asked, narrowing his eyes at me. "We're going to have a pleasant conversation."

I sighed and rolled my eyes. "Fine. But if he puts his hand on that Taser, we're going to have a problem."

"Yeah, well, if you'd stayed out of my murder investigation in the first place, we never would have had a problem," Liam said.

Jake glared at him. He didn't seem particularly

impressed with his partner's attempt at extending an olive branch.

"We need your version of what happened," Jake told me. "For the investigation."

"Rosie isn't going to be arrested, is she?" I asked. "After all, Alice was trying to kill us."

Jake nodded. "We heard. I can't say for sure, because it's not up to me, but we'll be recommending to the district attorney that this be declared a textbook case of self-defense."

"I don't like that we only have their word for it," Liam muttered.

I glared at him. "And I don't like the way your eyes are too close to each other, but you don't see me complaining. Fact is, Alice drugged us at the restaurant, forced us at gunpoint into her car, drove us into the middle of nowhere, and was going to kill us. I puked on her, which surprised her, and Rosie broke her neck. End of story."

"How did your friend know how to break a woman's neck? That's not exactly something most people know how to do," Liam asked.

"She's seen movies?" I offered with a shrug. "And she probably got lucky. We all got lucky. What do you think, she's some sort of ex-CIA agent?"

Liam looked uncomfortable. "No, of course not. That's ridiculous."

"That's right, it *is* ridiculous. We were just lucky it worked."

"You *were* lucky," Jake said. "I thought you said you weren't going to be investigating this case anymore."

"Whoops, I told a little white lie," I replied.

"You're impossible," Jake sighed.

"Sure, but I found your killer for you. You should be thanking me."

"With the amount of paperwork I'm going to have to do to deal with this, absolutely not," Jake replied. "We were onto Alice. We knew it was her. We just didn't have proof."

"Well, you should now," I replied. "Dot was recording the entire conversation between us. When we were in the car, Alice admitted to everything."

Jake nodded. "Rosie told us. We have Dot's phone and the recording. Not that it matters anymore, what with Alice being dead. She'll never pay for what she did to James MacMahon."

"Well, I'm not exactly going to shed a tear over the guy, either," I replied. After all, it wasn't as if he was the world's most innocent man. From what Alice had said, he used money to get away from harassment charges—if not worse.

Jake shrugged. "Either way, the case is closed now."

"The resort will still move ahead, in all likelihood," I countered.

"That's true. Unless someone finds that bribe money. I'm not keeping my hopes up, though."

"Me neither."

"All right, well, thanks for the statement. We'll be in touch if we need anything else." A soft expression came across Jake's face for a moment, as if he wanted to ask if I was all right. But he was interrupted by his partner.

"Come on, Jake. We're going to spend three days

doing all the paperwork thanks to these idiots and their vigilante work."

"You're welcome," I shouted to Liam's back, flipping him off as he left. If there was any justice in the world, he would Taser himself next time. Hopefully in the dick.

THREE WEEKS LATER, I CHECKED THE MAIL AND found a letter from New York, addressed to me. I opened it to find a check for a hundred thousand dollars in it.

I almost fainted just looking at it.

I immediately called Dot and Rosie and met them at the Starbucks where we'd had our first encounter. "I need your bank account details," I explained. "The check is in my name, so I'll deposit it and send you your share."

Rosie shook her head. "No, dear. Dot and I discussed it. The reason it's in your name alone is because we want you to have all of it."

My mouth dropped open. "What?"

"You were the one who figured out Alice was the killer," Dot said. "Besides, Rosie and I are old. We've had a lifetime of earning money. We have good pensions, we're financially stable, and frankly, we did it for the adventure more than we did for the money. You, on the other hand…"

When Dot trailed off, I finished the sentence for her. "Am a financial train wreck?"

"Well, I wasn't going to put it *quite* that way," Dot

replied. "But let's just say we both know you could use the money more than we can. This should help you find a place to live away from your mother."

A lump rose in my throat. "Thank you," I managed to say. Their kindness meant more than I could put into words.

"You deserve it," Rosie replied, reaching across and placing a hand on mine.

I was touched in a way I couldn't put into words. This was life-changing money, and they were giving it to me. My mind was made up: I was staying on Maui. There was no doubt about it.

BOOK 2 - MAUI MURDER: CHARLIE FINALLY FEELS like she's got a bit of breathing room. She's flush with cash, she and Zoe are moving into a snazzy new apartment, and she's riding the wave of having solved a murder a few weeks earlier. But when a local woman is murdered and her family hires Charlie to find the killer, she finds herself embroiled in yet another investigation.

However, what Charlie initially thinks might be an easy solve quickly finds her mired in Maui's seedy underworld, with a victim who led a double life. Finding herself dealing with a suspect list longer than a CVS receipt, Charlie enlists the help of Dot and Rosie to narrow down that list and get a lead on the real killer.

But between Jake trying to keep her out of the investigation, new neighbors who make Ozzy Osbourne look normal, and an attempted robbery at her day job,

Charlie quickly finds she's got her hands full once again. And to make matters worse, as Charlie gets closer to solving the crime, she realizes the killer has another target in mind: her.

Can Charlie bring another killer to justice before she's turned into shark bait?

Click here to read Maui Murder now.

About the Author

Jasmine Webb is a thirty-something who lives in the mountains most of the year, dreaming of the beach. When she's not writing stories you can find her chasing her old dog around, hiking up moderately-sized hills, or playing Pokemon Go.

Sign up for Jasmine's newsletter to be the first to find out about new releases here: http://www.authorjasminewebb.com/newsletter

You can also join Jasmine's Facebook Reader group here: http://www.facebook.com/groups/jasminewebb

You can also connect with her on other social media here:

A Note from the Author

Hi! I just wanted to say thank you for reading Aloha Alibi. I really hope you enjoyed this book, because I had a blast writing it.

If you'd like to help other readers find this book as well, please consider leaving a review on Amazon or Goodreads, or on whatever platform you purchased this book.

I have plenty of stories for Charlie and friends coming up in the future, but for now I highly recommend you check out Maui Murder, the next book in this series.

Until next time, I hope you're able to enjoy some sunshine, and that every book you read brings you unhinged joy.

Jasmine

Also by Jasmine Webb

Charlotte Gibson Mysteries

Aloha Alibi

Maui Murder

Beachside Bullet (Coming November 2020)

Made in the USA
Columbia, SC
03 November 2024

45594023R00162